Author, poet and translator, **Deepa Agarwal** writes for both children and adults and has about fifty published books to her credit. She has received several awards for her work. The picture book, *Ashok's New Friends*, was awarded the National Award for Children's Literature by the National Council of Educational Research and Training while her historical fiction, *Caravan to Tibet*, featured in the International Board on Books for Young People Honor List of 2008. Five of her titles have also been listed in the White Raven Catalogue of the International Youth Library, Munich.

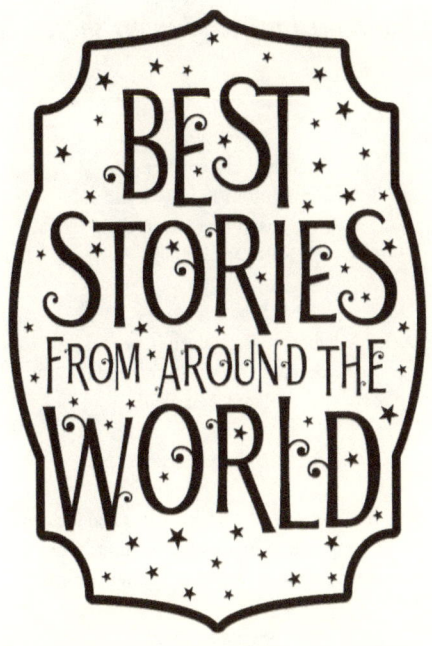

BEST STORIES FROM AROUND THE WORLD

Edited by Deepa Agarwal

RED TURTLE

RUPA

To my mother, Nancy Rawat,
who introduced me to so many short stories

Published in Red Turtle by
Rupa Publications India Pvt. Ltd 2017
7/16, Ansari Road, Daryaganj
New Delhi 110002

Sales centres:
Allahabad Bengaluru Chennai
Hyderabad Jaipur Kathmandu
Kolkata Mumbai

ISBN: 978-81-291-4738-7

First impression 2017

10 9 8 7 6 5 4 3 2 1

Printed and bound in India by Repro Knowledgecast Limited, Thane

Contents

Introduction

ONCE UPON a time there was a story. The child who read it was so enchanted that she/he couldn't stop at just one and kept searching for more and more. And what did that child discover? That there is no end to the number of stories you can devour with pleasure, because so many different kinds of stories have been written by so many authors at different times and in different places, all over the wide world.

What kinds of stories? Fairy tales and fantasies that will carry you off to imaginary worlds. Stories about real life events. Stories set in times past but also in the living present. Then detective stories that will make you bite your nails in suspense, and ghost stories that send a delicious shiver up your spine. There are funny stories that make you chuckle, but also stories that make you flare up with anger or shed a tear because they point out what is sadly wrong in our world. Some are about the essential goodness of human beings that remains unchanged in the worst of times, but some show us that dishonesty and cruelty exist alongside and that sometimes it's hard to recognize right from wrong. Some stories warm your heart, some make you think and some delight you with their magical language and enthral you with the extraordinary characters that people them or the gripping events that they unfold.

There is so much variety in the universe of stories that putting together this collection posed a bit of a challenge for me. So how did I tackle it? The easiest part was to travel back in time to dig up old favourites, of course, but it was extremely exciting to reach across the world to search for new ones. It was also a wonderful journey in reading because I discovered so many stories. Some told me about places and ways of life quite unfamiliar to me and some brought up issues and ideas that I had not thought deeply about before. So, in my attempt to put together a potpourri of stories that children with different tastes in reading might enjoy, I gained a lot.

How does one define a short story? There are many aspects to it, but I rather like what pioneering American short story writer Edgar Allan Poe had said in his essay 'The Philosophy of Composition,' that you should be able to read it in one sitting, anywhere from a half hour to two hours. That is the beauty of a short story, I feel. It can help you to fill up a short empty space in your day very enjoyably—whether it's while waiting for your turn at a dentist's or to catch a flight at an airport, without the frustration you experience when you have to abandon a gripping novel at the height of the action.

Our tastes in reading vary, as I mentioned earlier. Keeping this in mind, I've tried to make sure that you can flip the pages of this book and find a story that belongs to your favourite genre or suits your current mood.

If you are looking for a story that transports you beyond the mundane realities of our daily life you can go for Washington Irving's 'Rip Van Winkle'. It's a story I loved as a child and have re-read many times as an adult. And it's not just the possibility that supernatural beings might exist or a man can go to sleep for twenty years that always draws me, but the lovable character of Rip Van Winkle. Many of us know people like him, men who shirk regular work but are always there to help which makes them very popular with their neighbours. Said to be inspired by a folktale, this story is considered an all-time classic and with good reason.

'The Selfish Giant' by Oscar Wilde is also set outside the bounds of our reality—a fairy tale that carries a hidden meaning like many such tales do. It touched me deeply because it is a story of transformation and shows how children can melt even the stony heart of a self-centred man. Best of all, this change ultimately leads to his salvation. Talking about fairy tales, how could I leave out one of Hans Christian Andersen's well-loved classics? I have chosen 'The Brave Tin Soldier', a tender story written by one of the best writers for children in the world ever. There is often a deep vein of sadness in Andersen's stories that probably reflects the hardships he faced in his own childhood. But we can admire the steadfastness of the one-legged tin soldier, whose love for the paper ballerina shines bright through all his troubles.

It would be hard to put together a collection of memorable stories without including one of O. Henry's masterpieces. So we have 'The Gift of the Magi', a heart-warming Christmas story, an enduring narrative of devotion and sacrifice with the usual twist in the tale that was his trademark.

These are tales that move our hearts, but the stories in this book explore all kinds of themes and arouse a gamut of responses.

'Freedom' by Margaret Bhatty pitilessly exposes the corruption that has infected our system of law enforcement, when an old man with Gandhian ideals receives a criminal's punishment, only because he cannot abandon the values dear to him. We need such stories more than ever today, you might agree. 'The Dare' by South African writer Beverly Naidoo is a moving story about peer pressure. It highlights the brutality of a racist society while subtly weaving in a young girl's gesture of protest, a small gesture, but meaningful in its own way. Minoo Karimzadeh's 'The Last Ticket' transports us to Iran. The tale of young Sohrab's struggle with financial hardship when his family moves to a city is also a heartening portrayal of the empathy that is spontaneously aroused when we encounter someone who is worse off than us. In a sense, the last two stories I mentioned are coming of age, or growing up tales. So is 'The Minikin-Eared Ewe' by Tsendyin Damdinsüren that is set in the steppes of Mongolia, where a young boy battles the elements—a raging fire that he is ill-equipped to deal with. The author weaves a rich tapestry of the herdsmen's way of life and narrates the story of the boy's helplessness with a depth of feeling. We feel privileged to enter an environment quite unknown to us, and discover the challenges youngsters in other parts of the world face.

H.G. Wells's time-honoured favourite 'The Red Room' is guaranteed to raise a rash of goosebumps. The setting is traditionally spooky—a haunted castle, and the cast of characters just what you would expect to inhabit such a place. But the other ghost story—Jerry Pinto's 'Sarita Kamakshi Makes a Mistake' will grab your attention in a completely different manner—with its playful humour. The deftly sketched range of characters that prance through this very contemporary haunting are quite unique to Mumbai and the ending will definitely bring a smile to your face.

For Sherlock Holmes buffs, we have 'The Red-Headed League' one of Arthur Conan Doyle's gems, with the inimitable detective in full form. Layer upon layer of intrigue unfolds, keeping the reader glued to the page till the startling denouement arrives. Emile Gaboriau's hilarious 'The Accursed House', which wittily explores the theme of being too generous for your own good, is a very different kind of story. Interestingly, this French writer had created a famous detective character Monsieur Lecoq, whose popularity it is said, was somewhat eclipsed when Sherlock Holmes arrived on the scene.

How could I leave out one of my favourite short stories, a wickedly funny one, 'The Open Window' by Saki? Hector Hugh Munro, the British author, who wrote under this pen name is universally acknowledged as one of the masters of this form and his unique brand of humour is evident here in one of his most popular works. The Brer Rabbit stories too, were a memorable part of my growing up experience and I could not resist adding 'Brother Rabbit's Cradle' by Joel

Chandler Harris. If you can stay with the dialect, you will be rewarded with a delightful trickster tale which springs from African folklore. The author heard these stories from slaves in southern United States when he was young and decided to preserve these unique tales for posterity, creating the character Uncle Remus, who narrates them.

There is one more story I must mention, 'Valia' by Russian writer Leonid Andreiev, a leading literary figure who died about a hundred years ago. It is not a light-hearted tale but one that shows deep understanding of the heart of a child. Sensitive, bookish Valia is suddenly confronted with a traumatic change in his life. He displays great delicacy of feeling when he decides to accept it and thus wins our admiration.

There were many other stories I would have liked to include. But the limitations of space and other issues like permissions had to be kept in mind. All the same, I feel we have managed to put together a wide range of stories for you, each with a voice of its own, its own values, and its own kind of wisdom. Whether you read them in one go or dip into them at intervals, you will be rewarded with a distinctive experience. So...get ready to take a world tour, go time travelling and meet many memorable characters on the way!

Deepa Agarwal

The Selfish Giant

Oscar Wilde

Every afternoon, as they were coming from school, the children used to go and play in the Giant's garden.

It was a large lovely garden, with soft green grass. Here and there over the grass stood beautiful flowers like stars, and there were twelve peach-trees that in the spring-time broke out into delicate blossoms of pink and pearl, and in the Autumn bore rich fruit. The birds sat on the trees and sang so sweetly that the children used to stop their games in order to listen to them. 'How happy we are here!' they cried to each other.

One day the Giant came back. He had been to visit his friend the Cornish ogre, and had stayed with him for seven years. After the seven years were over he had said all that he had to say, for his conversation was limited, and he determined to return to his own castle. When he arrived, he saw the children playing in the garden.

'What are you doing here?' he cried in a very gruff voice, and the children ran away.

'My own garden is my own garden,' said the Giant; 'any one can understand that, and I will allow nobody to play in it but myself.' So he built a high wall all round it, and put up a noticeboard.

TRESPASSERS
WILL BE
PROSECUTED

He was a very selfish Giant.

The poor children had now nowhere to play. They tried to play on the road, but the road was very dusty and full of hard stones, and they did not like it. They used to wander round the high wall when their lessons were over, and talk about the beautiful garden inside.

'How happy we were there,' they said to each other.

Then the Spring came, and all over the country there were little blossoms and little birds. Only in the garden of the Selfish Giant it was still Winter. The birds did not care to sing in it as there were no children, and the trees forgot to blossom. Once a beautiful flower put its head out from the grass, but when it saw the noticeboard it was so sorry for the children that it slipped back into the ground again, and went off to sleep. The only people who were pleased were the Snow and the Frost. 'Spring has forgotten this garden,' they cried, 'so we will live here all the year round.' The Snow covered up the grass with her great white cloak, and the Frost painted all the trees silver. Then they invited the North Wind to stay with them, and he came. He was wrapped in furs, and he roared all day about the garden, and blew the chimney-pots down. 'This is a delightful spot,' he said, 'we must ask the Hail on a visit.' So the Hail came. Every day for three hours he rattled on the roof of the castle till he broke most of the slates, and then he ran round and round the garden as fast as he could go. He was dressed in grey, and his breath was like ice.

'I cannot understand why the Spring is so late in coming,' said the Selfish Giant, as he sat at the window and looked out at his cold white garden; 'I hope there will be a change in the weather.'

But the Spring never came, nor the Summer. The Autumn gave golden fruit to every garden, but to the Giant's garden she gave none. 'He is too selfish,' she said. So it was always Winter there, and the North Wind, and the Hail, and the Frost, and the Snow danced about through the trees.

One morning the Giant was lying awake in bed when he heard some lovely music. It sounded so sweet to his ears that he thought it must be the King's musicians passing by. It was really only a little linnet singing outside his window, but it was so long since he had heard a bird sing in his garden that it seemed to him to be the most beautiful music in the world. Then the Hail stopped dancing over his head, and the North Wind ceased roaring, and a delicious perfume came to him through the open casement. 'I believe Spring has come at last,' said the Giant; and he jumped out of bed and looked out.

What did he see?

He saw a most wonderful sight. Through a little hole in the wall the children had crept in, and they were sitting in the branches of the trees. In every tree that he could see there was a little child. And the trees were so glad to have the children back again that they had covered themselves with blossoms, and were waving their arms gently above the children's heads. The birds were flying about and twittering with delight, and the flowers were looking up through the green grass and laughing. It was a lovely scene, only in one corner it was still Winter. It was the farthest corner of the garden, and in it was standing a little boy. He was so small that he could not reach up to the branches of the tree, and he was wandering all round it, crying bitterly. The poor tree was still quite covered with frost and snow, and the North Wind was blowing and roaring above it. 'Climb up! little boy,' said the Tree, and it bent its branches down as low as it could; but the little boy was too tiny.

And the Giant's heart melted as he looked out. 'How selfish I have been!' he said; 'now I know why the Spring would not come here. I will put that poor little boy on top of the tree, and then I will knock down the wall, and my garden shall be the children's playground for ever and ever.' He was really very sorry for what he had done.

So he crept downstairs and opened the front door quite softly, and went out into the garden. But when the children saw him they were so frightened that they all ran away, and the garden became Winter again. Only the little boy did not run, for his eyes were so full of tears that he did not see the Giant coming. And the Giant stole up behind him and took him gently in his hand, and put him up into the tree. And the tree broke at once into blossom, and the birds came and sang on it, and the little boy stretched out his two arms and flung them round the Giant's neck, and kissed him. And the other children, when they saw that the Giant was not wicked any longer, came running back, and with them came the Spring. 'It is your garden now, little children,' said the Giant, and he took a great axe and knocked down the wall. And then the people going to market at twelve o'clock found the Giant playing with the children in the most beautiful garden they had ever seen.

All day long they played, and in the evening they came to the Giant to bid him goodbye.

'But where is your little companion?' he said: 'the boy I put into the tree.' The Giant loved him the best because he had kissed him.

'We don't know,' answered the children; 'he has gone away.'

'You must tell him to be sure and come here tomorrow,' said the Giant. But the children said that they did not know where he lived, and had never seen him before; and the Giant felt very sad.

Every afternoon, when school was over, the children came and played with the Giant. But the little boy whom the Giant loved was never seen again. The Giant was very kind to all the children, yet he longed for his first little friend, and often spoke of him. 'How I would like to see him!' he used to say.

Years went over, and the Giant grew very old and feeble. He could not play about any more, so he sat in a huge armchair, and watched the children at their games, and admired his garden. 'I have many beautiful flowers,' he said; 'but the children are the most beautiful flowers of all.'

One winter morning he looked out of his window as he was dressing. He did not hate the Winter now, for he knew that it was merely the Spring asleep, and that the flowers were resting.

Suddenly he rubbed his eyes in wonder, and looked and looked. It certainly was a marvellous sight. In the farthest corner of the garden was a tree quite covered with lovely white blossoms. Its branches were all golden, and silver fruit hung down from them, and underneath it stood the little boy he had loved.

Downstairs ran the Giant in great joy, and out into the garden. He hastened across the grass, and came near to the child. And when he came quite close his face grew red with anger, and he said, 'Who hath dared to wound thee?' For on the palms of the child's hands were the prints of two nails, and the prints of two nails were on his little feet.

'Who hath dared to wound thee?' cried the Giant; 'tell me, that I may take my big sword and slay him.'

'Nay!' answered the child; 'but these are the wounds of Love.'

'Who art thou?' said the Giant, and a strange awe fell on him, and he knelt before the little child.

And the child smiled on the Giant, and said to him, 'You let me play once in your garden, today you shall come with me to my garden, which is Paradise.'

And when the children ran in that afternoon, they found the Giant lying dead under the tree, all covered with white blossoms.

The Gift of the Magi

O. Henry

ONE DOLLAR and eighty-seven cents. That was all. And sixty cents of it was in pennies. Pennies saved one and two at a time by bulldozing the grocer and the vegetable man and the butcher until one's cheeks burned with the silent imputation of parsimony that such close dealing implied. Three times Della counted it. One dollar and eighty-seven cents. And the next day would be Christmas.

There was clearly nothing left to do but flop down on the shabby little couch and howl. So Della did it. Which instigates the moral reflection that life is made up of sobs, sniffles and smiles, with sniffles predominating.

While the mistress of the home is gradually subsiding from the first stage to the second, take a look at the home. A furnished flat at $8 per week. It did not exactly beggar description, but it certainly had that word on the lookout for the mendicancy squad.

In the vestibule below was a letter box into which no letter would go, and an electric button from which no mortal finger could coax a ring. Also appertaining thereunto was a card bearing the name 'Mr James Dillingham Young.'

The 'Dillingham' had been flung to the breeze during a former period of prosperity when its possessor was being paid $30 per week. Now, when the income was shrunk to $20, the letters of 'Dillingham' looked blurred, as though they were thinking seriously of contracting to a modest and unassuming D. But whenever Mr James Dillingham Young came home and reached his flat above he was called 'Jim' and greatly hugged by Mrs James Dillingham Young, already introduced to you as Della. Which is all very good.

Della finished her cry and attended to her cheeks with the powder rag. She stood by the window and looked out dully at a grey cat walking a grey fence in a grey backyard. Tomorrow would be Christmas Day, and she had only $1.87 with which to buy Jim a present. She had been saving every penny she could for months, with this result. Twenty dollars a week doesn't go far. Expenses had been greater than she had calculated. They always are. Only $1.87 to buy a present for Jim. Her Jim. Many a happy hour she had spent planning for something nice for him. Something fine and rare and sterling—something just a little bit near to being worthy of the honour of being owned by Jim.

There was a pier-glass between the windows of the room. Perhaps you have seen a pier-glass in an $8 flat. A very thin and agile person may, by observing his reflection in a rapid sequence of longitudinal strips, obtain a fairly accurate conception of his looks. Della, being slender, had mastered the art.

Suddenly she whirled from the window and stood before the glass. Her eyes were shining brilliantly, but her face had lost its colour within twenty seconds. Rapidly she pulled down her hair and let it fall to its full length.

Now, there were two possessions of the James Dillingham Youngs in which they both took a mighty pride. One was Jim's gold watch that had been his father's and his grandfather's. The other was Della's hair. Had the Queen of Sheba lived in the flat across the airshaft, Della would have let her hair hang out of the window some day to dry just to depreciate Her Majesty's jewels and gifts. Had King Solomon been the janitor, with all his treasures piled up in the basement, Jim would have pulled out his watch every time he passed, just to see him pluck at his beard from envy.

So now Della's beautiful hair fell about her, rippling and shining like a cascade of brown waters. It reached below her knee and made itself almost a garment for her. And then she did it up again nervously and quickly. Once she faltered for a minute and stood still while a tear or two splashed on the worn red carpet.

On went her old brown jacket; on went her old brown hat. With a whirl of skirts and with the brilliant sparkle still in her eyes, she cluttered out of the door and down the stairs to the street.

Where she stopped the sign read: 'Mme Sofronie. Hair Goods of All Kinds.' One flight up Della ran, and collected herself, panting. Madame, large, too white, chilly, hardly looked the 'Sofronie.'

'Will you buy my hair?' asked Della.

'I buy hair,' said Madame. 'Take yer hat off and let's have a sight at the looks of it.'

Down rippled the brown cascade.

'Twenty dollars,' said Madame, lifting the mass with a practised hand.

'Give it to me quick,' said Della.

Oh, and the next two hours tripped by on rosy wings. Forget the hashed metaphor. She was ransacking the stores for Jim's present.

She found it at last. It surely had been made for Jim and no one else. There was no other like it in any of the stores, and she had turned all of them inside out. It was a platinum fob chain simple and chaste in design, properly proclaiming its value by substance alone and not by meretricious ornamentation—as all good things should do. It was even worthy of The Watch. As soon as she saw it, she knew that it must be Jim's. It was like him. Quietness and value—the description applied to both. Twenty-one dollars they took from her for it, and she hurried home with the 78 cents. With that chain on his watch Jim might be properly anxious about the time in any company. Grand as the watch was, he sometimes looked at it on the sly on account of the old leather strap that he used in place of a chain.

When Della reached home her intoxication gave way a little to prudence and reason. She got out her curling irons and lighted the gas and went to work repairing the ravages made by generosity added to love. Which is always a tremendous task dear friends—a mammoth task.

Within forty minutes her head was covered with tiny, close-lying curls that made her look wonderfully like a truant schoolboy. She looked at her reflection in the mirror long, carefully, and critically.

'If Jim doesn't kill me,' she said to herself, 'before he takes a second look at me, he'll say I look like a Coney Island chorus girl. But what could I do—oh! What could I do with a dollar and eighty-seven cents?'

At 7 o'clock the coffee was made and the frying pan was on the back of the stove, hot and ready, to cook the chops.

Jim was never late. Della doubled the fob chain in her hand and sat on the corner of the table near the door that he always entered. Then she heard his step on the stair away down on the first flight, and she turned white for just a moment. She had a habit of saying little silent prayers about the simplest everyday things, and now she whispered: 'Please, God, make him think I am still pretty.'

The door opened and Jim stepped in and closed it. He looked thin and very serious. Poor fellow, he was only twenty-two—and to be burdened with a family! He needed a new overcoat and he was without gloves.

Jim stepped inside the door, as immovable as a setter at the scent of quail. His eyes were fixed upon Della, and there was an expression in them that she could not read, and it terrified her. It was not anger, nor surprise, nor disapproval, nor horror, nor any of the sentiments that she had been prepared for. He simply stared at her fixedly with that peculiar expression on his face.

Della wriggled off the table and went for him.

'Jim, darling,' she cried, 'don't look at me that way. I had my hair cut off and sold it because I couldn't have lived through Christmas without giving you a present. It'll grow out again—you won't mind, will you? I just had to do it. My hair grows awfully fast. Say 'Merry Christmas!' Jim, and let's be happy. You don't know what a nice–what a beautiful, nice gift I've got for you.'

'You've cut off your hair?' asked Jim, labouriously, as if he had not arrived at that patent fact yet, even after the hardest mental labour.

'Cut it off and sold it,' said Della. 'Don't you like me just as well, anyhow? I'm me without my hair, ain't I?'

Jim looked about the room curiously.

'You say your hair is gone?' he said, with an air almost of idiocy.

'You needn't look for it,' said Della. 'It's sold, I tell you— sold and gone, too. It's Christmas Eve, boy. Be good to me, for it went for you. Maybe the hair of my head were numbered,' she went on with a sudden serious sweetness, 'but nobody could ever count my love for you. Shall I put the chops on, Jim?'

Out of his trance Jim seemed quickly to wake. He enfolded his Della. For ten seconds let us regard with discreet scrutiny some inconsequential object in the other direction. Eight dollars a week or a million a year—what is the difference? A mathematician or a wit would give you the wrong answer. The magi brought valuable gifts, but that was not among them. This dark assertion will be illuminated later on.

Jim drew a package from his overcoat pocket and threw it upon the table.

'Don't make any mistake, Dell,' he said, 'about me. I don't think there's anything in the way of a haircut or a shave or a shampoo that could make me like my girl any less. But if you'll unwrap that package you may see why you had me going a while at first.'

White and nimble fingers tore at the string and paper. And then an ecstatic scream of joy; and then, alas! a quick feminine change to hysterical tears and wails, necessitating the immediate employment of all the comforting powers of the lord of the flat.

For there lay The Combs—the set of combs, side and back, that Della had worshipped for long in a Broadway window. Beautiful combs, pure tortoise-shell, with jewelled rims—just the shade to wear in the beautiful vanished hair. They were expensive combs, she knew, and her heart had simply craved and yearned over them without the least hope of possession. And now, they were hers, but the tresses that should have adorned the coveted adornments were gone.

But she hugged them to her bosom, and at length she was able to look up with dim eyes and a smile and say: 'My hair grows so fast, Jim!'

And then Della leaped up like a little singed cat and cried, 'Oh, oh!'

Jim had not yet seen his beautiful present. She held it out to him eagerly upon her open palm. The dull precious metal seemed to flash with a reflection of her bright and ardent spirit.

'Isn't it a dandy, Jim? I hunted all over town to find it.

You'll have to look at the time a hundred times a day now. Give me your watch. I want to see how it looks on it.'

Instead of obeying, Jim tumbled down on the couch and put his hands under the back of his head and smiled.

'Dell,' said he, 'let's put our Christmas presents away and keep 'em a while. They're too nice to use just at present. I sold the watch to get the money to buy your combs. And now suppose you put the chops on.'

The magi, as you know, were wise men—wonderfully wise men—who brought gifts to the Babe in the manger. They invented the art of giving Christmas presents. Being wise, their gifts were no doubt wise ones, possibly bearing the privilege of exchange in case of duplication. And here I have lamely related to you the uneventful chronicle of two foolish children in a flat who most unwisely sacrificed for each other the greatest treasures of their house. But in a last word to the wise of these days let it be said that of all who give gifts these two were the wisest. Of all who give and receive gifts, such as they are wisest. Everywhere they are wisest. They are the magi.

The Open Window

Saki

'My aunt will be down presently, Mr Nuttel,' said a very self-possessed young lady of fifteen; 'in the meantime you must try and put up with me.'

Framton Nuttel endeavoured to say the correct something which should duly flatter the niece of the moment without unduly discounting the aunt that was to come. Privately, he doubted more than ever, whether these formal visits on a succession of total strangers would do much towards helping the nerve cure which he was supposed to be undergoing.

'I know how it will be,' his sister had said when he was preparing to migrate to this rural retreat; 'you will bury yourself down there and not speak to a living soul, and your nerves will be worse than ever from moping. I shall just give you letters of introduction to all the people I know there. Some of them, as far as I can remember, were quite nice.'

Framton wondered whether Mrs Sappleton, the lady to

whom he was presenting one of the letters of introduction, came into the nice division.

'Do you know many of the people round here?' asked the niece, when she judged that they had had sufficient silent communion.

'Hardly a soul,' said Framton. 'My sister was staying here, at the rectory, you know, some four years ago, and she gave me letters of introduction to some of the people here.'

He made the last statement in a tone of distinct regret.

'Then you know practically nothing about my aunt?' pursued the self-possessed young lady.

'Only her name and address,' admitted the caller. He was wondering whether Mrs Sappleton was in the married or widowed state. An undefinable something about the room seemed to suggest masculine habitation.

'Her great tragedy happened just three years ago,' said the child; 'that would be since your sister's time.'

'Her tragedy?' asked Framton; somehow in this restful country spot tragedies seemed out of place.

'You may wonder why we keep that window wide open on an October afternoon,' said the niece, indicating a large French window that opened on to a lawn.

'It is quite warm for the time of the year,' said Framton; 'but has that window got anything to do with the tragedy?'

'Out through that window, three years ago to a day, her husband and her two young brothers went off for their day's shooting. They never came back. In crossing the moor to their favourite snipe-shooting ground they were all three engulfed in a treacherous piece of bog. It had been that dreadful wet summer, you know, and places that were safe in other years gave way suddenly without warning. Their bodies were never recovered. That was the dreadful part of it.' Here the child's voice lost its self-possessed note and became falteringly human. 'Poor aunt always thinks that they will come back someday, they and the little brown spaniel that was lost with them, and walk in at that window just as they used to do. That is why the window is kept open every evening till it is quite dusk. Poor dear aunt, she has often told me how they went out, her husband with his white waterproof coat over his arm, and Ronnie, her youngest brother, singing 'Bertie, why do you bound?' as he always did to tease her, because she said it got on her nerves. Do you know, sometimes on still, quiet evenings like this, I almost get a creepy feeling that they will all walk in through that window—'

She broke off with a little shudder. It was a relief to Framton when the aunt bustled into the room with a whirl of apologies for being late in making her appearance.

'I hope Vera has been amusing you?' she said.

'She has been very interesting,' said Framton.

'I hope you don't mind the open window,' said Mrs Sappleton briskly; 'my husband and brothers will be home directly from shooting, and they always come in this way. They've been out for snipe in the marshes today, so they'll make a fine mess over my poor carpets. So like you menfolk, isn't it?'

She rattled on cheerfully about the shooting and the scarcity of birds, and the prospects for duck in the winter. To Framton it was all purely horrible. He made a desperate but only partially successful effort to turn the talk on to a less ghastly topic, he was conscious that his hostess was giving him only a fragment of her attention, and her eyes were constantly straying past him to the open window and the lawn beyond. It was certainly an unfortunate coincidence that he should have paid his visit on this tragic anniversary.

'The doctors agree in ordering me complete rest, an absence of mental excitement, and avoidance of anything in the nature of violent physical exercise,' announced Framton, who laboured under the tolerably widespread delusion that total strangers and chance acquaintances are hungry for the least detail of one's ailments and infirmities, their cause and cure. 'On the matter of diet, they are not so much in agreement,' he continued.

'No?' said Mrs Sappleton, in a voice which only replaced a yawn at the last moment. Then she suddenly brightened into alert attention—but not to what Framton was saying.

'Here they are at last!' she cried. 'Just in time for tea, and don't they look as if they were muddy up to the eyes!'

Framton shivered slightly and turned towards the niece with a look intended to convey sympathetic comprehension. The child was staring out through the open window with a dazed horror in her eyes. In a chill shock of nameless fear Framton swung round in his seat and looked in the same direction.

In the deepening twilight three figures were walking across the lawn towards the window, they all carried guns under their arms, and one of them was additionally burdened with a white coat hung over his shoulders. A tired brown spaniel kept close at their heels. Noiselessly they neared the house, and then a hoarse young voice chanted out of the dusk: 'I said, Bertie, why do you bound?'

Framton grabbed wildly at his stick and hat; the hall door, the gravel drive, and the front gate were dimly noted stages in his headlong retreat. A cyclist coming along the road had to run into the hedge to avoid imminent collision.

'Here we are, my dear,' said the bearer of the white mackintosh, coming in through the window, 'fairly muddy, but most of it's dry. Who was that who bolted out as we came up?'

'A most extraordinary man, a Mr Nuttel,' said Mrs Sappleton; 'could only talk about his illnesses, and dashed off without a word of goodbye or apology when you arrived. One would think he had seen a ghost.'

'I expect it was the spaniel,' said the niece calmly; 'he told me he had a horror of dogs. He was once hunted into a cemetery somewhere on the banks of the Ganges by a pack of pariah dogs, and had to spend the night in a newly dug grave with the creatures snarling and grinning and foaming just above him. Enough to make anyone lose their nerve.'

Romance at short notice was her speciality.

The Brave Tin Soldier

Hans Christian Andersen

THERE WERE once five-and-twenty tin soldiers, who were all brothers, for they had been made out of the same old tin spoon. They shouldered arms and looked straight before them, and wore a splendid uniform, red and blue. The first thing in the world they ever heard were the words, 'Tin soldiers!' uttered by a little boy, who clapped his hands with delight when the lid of the box, in which they lay, was taken off. They were given to him for a birthday present, and he stood at the table to set them up. The soldiers were all exactly alike, excepting one, who had only one leg; he had been left to the last, and then there was not enough of the melted tin to finish him, so they made him to stand firmly on one leg, and this caused him to be very remarkable.

The table on which the tin soldiers stood, was covered with other playthings, but the most attractive to the eye was a pretty little paper castle. Through the small windows the rooms could be seen. In front of the castle a number of little trees surrounded a piece of looking glass, which was intended to represent a transparent lake. Swans, made of wax, swam on the lake, and were reflected in it. All this was very pretty, but the prettiest of all was a tiny little lady, who stood at the open door of the castle; she, also, was made of paper, and she wore a dress of clear muslin, with a narrow blue ribbon over her shoulders just like a scarf. In front of these was fixed a glittering tinsel rose, as large as her whole face. The little lady was a dancer, and she stretched out both her arms, and raised one of her legs so high, that the tin soldier could not see it at all, and he thought that she, like himself, had only one leg.

'That is the wife for me,' he thought; 'but she is too grand, and lives in a castle, while I have only a box to live in, five-and-twenty of us altogether, that is no place for her. Still I must try and make her acquaintance.' Then he laid himself at full length on the table behind a snuff-box that stood upon it, so that he could peep at the little delicate lady, who continued to stand on one leg without losing her balance.

When evening came, the other tin soldiers were all placed in the box, and the people of the house went to bed. Then the playthings began to have their own games together, to pay visits, to have sham fights, and to give balls. The tin soldiers rattled in their box; they wanted to get out and join the amusements, but they could not open the lid. The nut-crackers played at leap-frog, and the pencil jumped about the table. There was such a noise that the canary woke up and began to talk, and in poetry too. Only the tin soldier and the dancer remained in their places. She stood on tiptoe, with her legs stretched out, as firmly as he did on his one leg. He never took his eyes from her for even a moment. The clock struck twelve, and, with a bounce, up sprang the lid of the snuff-box; but, instead of snuff, there jumped up a little black goblin; for the snuff-box was a toy puzzle.

'Tin soldier,' said the goblin, 'don't wish for what does not belong to you.

But the tin soldier pretended not to hear.

'Very well; wait till tomorrow, then,' said the goblin.

When the children came in the next morning, they placed the tin soldier in the window. Now, whether it was the goblin who did it, or the draught, is not known, but the window flew open, and out fell the tin soldier, heels over head, from the third storey, into the street beneath. It was a terrible fall; for he came head downwards, his helmet and his bayonet stuck in between the flagstones, and his one leg up in the air. The servant maid and the little boy went downstairs directly to look for him; but he was nowhere to be seen, although once they nearly trod upon him. If he had called out, 'Here I am,' it would have been all right, but he was too proud to cry out for help while he wore a uniform.

Presently it began to rain, and the drops fell faster and faster, till there was a heavy shower. When it was over, two boys happened to pass by, and one of them said, 'Look, there is a tin soldier. He ought to have a boat to sail in.'

So they made a boat out of a newspaper, and placed the tin soldier in it, and sent him sailing down the gutter, while the two boys ran by the side of it, and clapped their hands. Good gracious, what large waves arose in that gutter! and how fast the stream rolled on! for the rain had been very heavy. The paper boat rocked up and down, and turned itself round sometimes so quickly that the tin soldier trembled; yet he remained firm; his countenance did not change; he looked straight before him, and shouldered his musket. Suddenly the boat shot under a bridge which formed part of a drain, and then it was as dark as the tin soldier's box.

'Where am I going now?' thought he. 'This is the black goblin's fault, I am sure. Ah, well, if the little lady were only here with me in the boat, I should not care for any darkness.'

Suddenly there appeared a great water-rat, who lived in the drain.

'Have you a passport?' asked the rat, 'give it to me at once.' But the tin soldier remained silent and held his musket tighter than ever. The boat sailed on and the rat followed it. How he did gnash his teeth and cry out to the bits of wood and straw, 'Stop him, stop him; he has not paid toll, and has not shown his pass.' But the stream rushed on stronger and stronger. The tin soldier could already see daylight shining where the arch ended. Then he heard a roaring sound quite terrible enough to frighten the bravest man. At the end of the tunnel the drain fell into a large canal over a steep place, which made it as dangerous for him as a waterfall would be to us. He was too close to it to stop, so the boat rushed on, and the poor tin soldier could only hold himself as stiffly as possible, without moving an eyelid, to show that he was not afraid. The boat whirled round three or four times, and then filled with water to the very edge; nothing could save it from sinking. He now stood up to his neck in water, while deeper and deeper sank the boat, and the paper became soft and loose with the wet, till at last the water closed over the soldier's head. He thought of the elegant little dancer whom he should never see again, and the words of the song sounded in his ears—

'Farewell, warrior! ever brave,

Drifting onward to thy grave.'—

Then the paper boat fell to pieces, and the soldier sank into the water and immediately afterwards was swallowed up by a great fish. Oh, how dark it was inside the fish! A great deal darker than in the tunnel, and narrower too, but the tin soldier continued firm, and lay at full length shouldering his musket. The fish swam to and fro, making the most wonderful movements, but at last he became quite still. After a while, a flash of lightning seemed to pass through him, and then the daylight approached, and a voice cried out, 'I declare here is the tin soldier.'

The fish had been caught, taken to the market and sold to the cook, who took him into the kitchen and cut him open with a large knife. She picked up the soldier and held him by the waist between her finger and thumb, and carried him into the room. They were all anxious to see this wonderful soldier who had travelled about inside a fish; but he was not at all proud. They placed him on the table, and how many curious things do happen in the world! There he was in the very same room from the window of which he had fallen, there were the same children, the same playthings, standing on the table, and the pretty castle with the elegant little dancer at the door; she still balanced herself on one leg, and held up the other, so she was as firm as himself. It touched the tin soldier so much to see her that he almost wept tin tears, but he kept them back. He only looked at her and they both remained silent.

Presently one of the little boys took up the tin soldier, and threw him into the stove. He had no reason for doing so, therefore it must have been the fault of the black goblin who lived in the snuff-box. The flames lighted up the tin soldier, as he stood, the heat was very terrible, but whether it proceeded from the real fire or from the fire of love he could not tell. Then he could see that the bright colours were faded from his uniform, but whether they had been washed off during his journey or from the effects of his sorrow, no one could say. He looked at the little lady, and she looked at him. He felt himself melting away, but he still remained firm with his gun on his shoulder. Suddenly the door of the room flew open and the draught of air caught up the little dancer, she fluttered like a sylph right into the stove by the side of the tin soldier, and was instantly in flames and was gone. The tin soldier melted down into a lump, and the next morning, when the maidservant took the ashes out of the stove, she found him in the shape of a little tin heart. But of the little dancer nothing remained but the tinsel rose, which was burnt black as a cinder.

Freedom

Margaret Bhatty

There were a number of things that sixty-year-old Shankarao did wrong that unlucky Wednesday. To begin with he didn't listen to his wife.

'Don't go to the city today,' said Laxmibai. 'Go tomorrow; then I can come too and we'll visit the Sai Baba Mandir.'

Shankarao replied that he had to go that very day because it was his only free evening. He had finished forging the six sickles ordered by the Patil and let his fire die out.

'Tomorrow I must do the rims for the two bullock cart wheels Panduarang Sutar left with me.'

'Don't go today,' Laxmibai insisted. 'My Bad Eye has been fluttering and those two crows in the neem have been laughing all afternoon in a peculiar manner.'

Shankarao pulled a crumpled kurta over his head and got into his shoes. He didn't change his dhoti. There was no time. He would miss the four o'clock bus if he didn't hurry. 'I want to get my watch cleaned and buy a new strap,' he said.

'You cannot go like that!' his wife protested. 'At least put on clean clothes.'

But he snatched his Gandhi cap off the nail on the wall and disappeared round the house. His cap was white and clean, but his clothes were his workday ones, with soot and scorch marks from his smithy fire.

If he went into the city today and left his watch at the Jubilee Watch House, he figured he would still have seven days to pick it up. It was his most prized possession, gifted to him years ago when he was a young man in his twenties and working at Sevagram Ashram. The donor had been a very wealthy businessman who had renounced the world and joined the ashram.

Shankarao was a freedom fighter, an unofficial one, since he drew no pension nor laid claim to such an honoured title. But Gandhiji had known him by name and he had worked for three years at Sevagram, teaching young pupils his craft as a blacksmith. He had faced bullets and lathis during the freedom struggle, and spent a few months in gaol off and on.

On one occasion, when the English governor of the Central Provinces had come to Nagpur to stay at the Government House, he was greeted by black flags. The crowd had turned unruly, and hurled shoes and slippers at his car. These slammed against its sides and fell on the road, or were knocked off the bonnet by his mounted escort. Only Shankarao's chappal remained on the roof and was borne along, all the way to the gate, where a policeman threw it aside. This was before Shankarao was converted to non-violence.

Nevertheless, it was a story he liked to relate. In fact, he had nailed the other chappal to the beam over his door. 'If need be, I will use this, too—against injustice, against anyone who tries to oppress my country.'

It was because of his record in the Freedom Movement that the village schoolmaster had asked Shankarao to be the guest of honour and hoist the tricolour at the Independence Day celebrations. Since they were celebrating forty years of freedom, the chief guest had to be a very special person. Shankarao was proud. He intended to make a speech on his watch and its significance to him, for there was an object lesson in it. But the watch needed a new strap.

Hurrying along the lane between the houses, he was hailed by a number of people. 'What's the hurry, Shankarao?'

He was going into the city, to the watch shop, he explained and would be back by the last bus at eight. 'Wait!' cried his old friend Govardhan. 'Take mine, too. It has stopped working altogether.'

By the time Shankarao reached the bus stop on the highway he had four watches, two strapped on each wrist, his own and three others to be given for repair. This was safer since his kurta pocket had a small hole. That was the simple explanation he gave Constable Sakaram, the man who arrested him.

Constable Sakaram was in a vile mood. He stood on the pavement at Liberty Square scowling at the office-hour traffic streaming past. He had been given a final warning by Sub-Inspector Ingole that afternoon for failing to do certain duties assigned to him, and for being drunk on his beat. If he didn't look out, Ingole said, he would be transferred away from the city. Sakaram's small mean eyes darted about as he stood leaning against the railing a few yards from the Jubilee Watch Shop. He saw the bus from the rural route stop opposite for passengers to alight. He saw an elderly scruffy, unshaved, slightly built, shabbily dressed fellow standing on the opposite side, nervously waiting for a break in the traffic to dash across. The man almost got run down by a truck, but he made it. Breathing hard, he drew level with Sakaram and raised his hands to settle his cap more firmly. His kurta sleeves fell away to reveal he was carrying loot—strapped on both wrists, too!

'Stop!' said Constable Sakaram, poking his baton into the man's stomach. 'What's this, huh?'

Shankarao smiled as the policeman pushed up his sleeves and stared at the watches. 'I've brought them for repairs,' he said. 'This is Govardhan's—it has stopped. This Gulab Tangliya's—the minute hand has fallen off. This is Vasudeo's—it doesn't keep good time. And this is mine.'

The Constable looked at the watches and then at Shankarao's clothes. The stories these rogues think up!

'Where did you steal them?' he snarled, taking hold of Shankar by the front of his kurta.

'Steal?' cried Shankarao. 'I am an honest man and have never stolen a thing in my life! Let me go, I say!'

In his panic he had raised his voice, making people turn and stare. Curious ones soon collected. The policeman held him hard and when Shankarao tried to push him off, his frayed kurta tore.

'Look at him!' cried the constable. 'Wristwatches on both

arms and he says he is an honest man!'

'Let me go! Let me go!' cried Shankarao, now truly afraid.

Helpful people in the crowd also took hold of him. He was marched off to the thana.

Sub-Inspector Ingole sat behind the desk and stared first at the prisoner, a shabby old crook, not a very smart one either, judging from his story. He then looked at the flabby, fish-faced Constable Sakaram beaming from ear to ear as he made his report.

'He resisted arrest, sah!' he said. 'And he tried to push me down, sah. He assaulted me, too.'

Ingole examined the watches placed before him, not listening to Shankarao's stammered protests. Three were cheap pieces; the fourth made him stare. Swiss-made. Six jewels. Old but well-preserved.

'That is mine, Inspector Sahib,' Shankarao said.

The officer looked him up and down, noticed his grimy clothes—his torn kurta and scorched old dhoti. And when he was told the name of the man who had presented it to Shankar, forty-one years ago at Sevagram, he laughed out loud. The name Shankar took was of one of the richest industrialists in the country.

'Every day people like you come in and tell me tall stories,' Ingole said sourly. 'Maybe a night in the lock up will help you remember better where you really got these watches. Take him away, Sakaram, and make your report. Shabaash!'

Back in the village Laxmibai heard the last bus stop by. But when Shankar didn't show up, she went over to Govardhan's who said he might have met a friend in the city and stayed on.

They waited three days for him, wondering how they could ever hope to locate a man in a city teeming with lakhs of people. Laxmibai had visions of her husband under a truck in a road accident. Assaulted and robbed by goondas. Afflicted by a sudden loss of memory and unable to remember who he was.

Govardhan, Tangliya and Vasudeo finally took a bus to the city. They went first to the Jubilee Watch Shop and asked if a man had come on Wednesday evening with four watches for repair.

The old proprietor scratched his chin and thought hard. Then he snapped his fingers. But yes, he said, there was some kind of incident right outside his shop—a policeman had arrested a shabby old fellow with wristwatches strapped all the way up his arms. Smuggled watches. Expensive ones. 'I didn't see him but that's what I heard the crowd say—'

They found Shankarao in the lock-up, confined with drunks and riff-raff. He was sitting in a corner, his head on his drawn-up knees. The rest was simple. They met Sub-Inspector Ingole, identified their watches, and vouched for the prisoner's record as an honest and upright man. There was no reason why Shankarao should be held any longer.

'Constable Sakaram, make out a receipt for these watches and the fellow's wallet,' Ingole ordered. 'But for resisting arrest, for assaulting a policeman, and for preventing him from doing his duty, fine him fifty rupees.'

Shankarao was aghast. 'He roughed me up because I am a poor man!' he cried. 'Had I been wearing suit-boot and dangling gold watches from my ears, would he have dared to manhandle me the way he did? What is my crime, then? Simply that I am poor? I will not pay! Do you hear?'

He had raised his voice without being aware of it, until he was shouting.

'Lower your voice!' Ingole snarled. 'Or I will make you lower it. How dare you shout at me? Constable, take him away and settle this business between yourselves.'

Outside the thana, off to one side and out of earshot of others, the policeman said, 'Arey bhai! This is a routine fine—you pay, you go free. That's all!'

Shankarao's friends began taking out their purses to make up the amount while the constable licked his thick lips and grinned. But Shankarao said, 'No! We must not pay. Do not ask me why, but we must not pay—'

'Then go and hire a lawyer,' sneered the constable. 'He'll fleece you—twenty times the amount. Maybe then you will be happy.' Thus it came about that Shankarao Khosare was not present to hoist the flag on the school ground on the fortieth year of freedom. He was in the police lock-up for a week in lieu of the fine he refused to pay because he believed it was dishonest.

He returned home almost by stealth, taking the last bus at eight, when it was dark, and walking soundlessly through the lanes, his head bent. No, he said, when Laxmibai asked if he had been ill-treated or beaten. And then he fell silent. When friends came in the morning to sit under his neem and share a hookah, he hardly spoke. They sympathized but there was nothing they could do. He had lost face and it would take time for the humiliation to wear off.

Shankarao didn't light his forge fire for two days. He sat brooding under the neem where the crows jeered and chortled above his head. He was consumed by a blind fury that seemed to fill him from top to toe, growing and growing until he couldn't breathe. At night he tossed and turned, his mind in turmoil. A great injustice had been done to him. But to whom should he turn for redress? His reputation was gone. The schoolchildren going past his aangan stared at him curiously; some whispered and pointed. Nobody believed he had done wrong. But there remained the stigma of his arrest and imprisonment.

Forty years ago he had also gone to gaol, making a courageous stand against injustice and oppression. He had done the same this time too, but somehow it had not afforded him the same sense of achievement or satisfaction. Somehow it had appalled him. He had to act. He had to demonstrate his protest and his anger.

He waited until Laxmibai was away at the well, washing clothes. Walking swiftly, he took a bus to the city. He carried a cloth bag with something in it. He felt resolute until he got to the gate of the police station. Then his nerve seemed to fail. Instead of marching in, head up, he crept almost furtively into the compound.

There were a few policemen standing about, along with ordinary people. He went round to the side of the building where there was a cycle-stand and parking for motorcycles. Taking out the slipper he had kept all these years—the pair to the one he had hurled at the angrez Governor's car—he looked at it for a long moment. His intention was to hurl it against the large signboard that said Gandhi Chowk Police Station. But his aim was not as good as it had been when he was in his twenties. He missed the board, missed the building. Instead, the chappal went flying across the entrance into the thana. It caught Sub-Inspector Ingole full on his face as he came round the corner to get to his motorcycle.

Everybody said it was a stupid, senseless, suicidal thing he did. 'He lives only in the past,' Laxmibai fumed. 'What did he think? The British Raj left because he threw one chappal? And the second chappal would make this Raj also go away? Old age has softened his brains.'

The magistrate awarded him three months' simple imprisonment.

The Red Room

H.G. Wells

'I can assure you,' said I, 'that it will take a very tangible ghost to frighten me.' And I stood up before the fire with my glass in my hand.

'It is your own choosing,' said the man with the withered arm, and glanced at me askance.

'Eight-and-twenty years,' said I, 'I have lived, and never a ghost have I seen as yet.' The old woman sat staring hard into the fire, her pale eyes wide open. 'Ay,' she broke in; 'and eight-and-twenty years you have lived and never seen the likes of this house, I reckon. There's a many things to see, when one's still but eight-and-twenty.' She swayed her head slowly from side to side. 'A many things to see and sorrow for.'

I half suspected the old people were trying to enhance the spiritual terrors of their house by their droning insistence. I put down my empty glass on the table and looked about the room, and caught a glimpse of myself, abbreviated and broadened to an impossible sturdiness, in the queer old mirror at the end of the room. 'Well,' I said, 'if I see anything tonight, I shall be so much the wiser. For I come to the business with an open mind.'

'It's your own choosing,' said the man with the withered arm once more.

I heard the sound of a stick and a shambling step on the flags in the passage outside, and the door creaked on its hinges as a second old man entered, more bent, more wrinkled, more aged even than the first. He supported himself by a single crutch, his eyes were covered by a shade, and his lower lip, half averted, hung pale and pink from his decaying yellow teeth. He made straight for an armchair on the opposite side of the table, sat down clumsily, and began to cough. The man with the withered arm gave this newcomer a short glance of positive dislike; the old woman took no notice of his arrival, but remained with her eyes fixed steadily on the fire.

'I said—it's your own choosing,' said the man with the withered arm, when the coughing had ceased for a while.

'It's my own choosing,' I answered.

The man with the shade became aware of my presence for the first time, and threw his head back for a moment and sideways, to see me. I caught a momentary glimpse of his eyes, small and bright and inflamed. Then he began to cough and splutter again.

'Why don't you drink?' said the man with the withered arm, pushing the beer towards him. The man with the shade poured out a glassful with a shaky hand that splashed half as much again on the deal table. A monstrous shadow of him crouched upon the wall and mocked his action as he poured and drank. I must confess I had scarcely expected these grotesque custodians. There is to my mind something inhuman in senility, something crouching and atavistic; the human qualities seem to drop from old people insensibly day by day. The three of them made me feel uncomfortable, with their gaunt silences, their bent carriage, their evident unfriendliness to me and to one another.

'If,' said I, 'you will show me to this haunted room of yours, I will make myself comfortable there.'

The old man with the cough jerked his head back so suddenly that it startled me, and shot another glance of his red eyes at me from under the shade; but no one answered me. I waited a minute, glancing from one to the other.

'If,' I said a little louder, 'if you will show me to this haunted room of yours, I will relieve you from the task of entertaining me.'

'There's a candle on the slab outside the door,' said the man with the withered arm, looking at my feet as he addressed me. 'But if you go to the red room tonight—'

'This night of all nights!' said the old woman.

'You go alone.'

'Very well,' I answered. 'And which way do I go?'

'You go along the passage for a bit,' said he, 'until you come to a door, and through that is a spiral staircase, and halfway up that is a landing and another door covered with baize. Go through that and down the long corridor to the end, and the red room is on your left up the steps.'

'Have I got that right?' I said, and repeated his directions.

He corrected me in one particular.

'And are you really going?' said the man with the shade, looking at me again for the third time, with that queer, unnatural tilting of the face.

'This night of all nights!' said the old woman.

'It is what I came for,' I said, and moved towards the door. As I did so, the old man with the shade rose and staggered round the table, so as to be close to the others and to the fire. At the door I turned and looked at them, and saw they were all close together, dark against the firelight, staring at me over their shoulders, with an intent expression on their ancient faces.

'Good night,' I said, setting the door open.

'It's your own choosing,' said the man with the withered arm.

I left the door wide open until the candle was well alight, and then I shut them in and walked down the chilly, echoing passage.

I must confess that the oddness of these three old pensioners in whose charge her ladyship had left the castle, and the deep-toned, old-fashioned furniture of the housekeeper's room in which they foregathered, affected me in spite of my efforts to keep myself at a matter-of-fact phase. They seemed to belong to another age, an older age, an age when things spiritual were different from this of ours, less certain; an age when omens and witches were credible, and ghosts beyond denying. Their very existence was spectral; the cut of their clothing, fashions born in dead brains. The ornaments and conveniences of the room about them were ghostly—the thoughts of vanished men, which still haunted rather than participated in the world of today. But with an effort I sent such thoughts to the right-about. The long, draughty subterranean passage was chilly and dusty, and my candle flared and made the shadows cower and quiver. The echoes rang up and down the spiral staircase, and a shadow came sweeping up after me, and one fled before me into the darkness overhead. I came to the landing and stopped there for a moment, listening to a rustling that I fancied I heard; then, satisfied of the absolute silence, I pushed open the baize-covered door and stood in the corridor.

The effect was scarcely what I expected, for the moonlight, coming in by the great window on the grand staircase, picked out everything in vivid black shadow or silvery illumination. Everything was in its place: the house might have been deserted on the yesterday instead of eighteen months ago. There were candles in the sockets of the sconces, and whatever dust had gathered on the carpets or upon the polished flooring was distributed so evenly as to be invisible in the moonlight. I was about to advance, and stopped abruptly. A bronze group stood upon the landing, hidden from me by the corner of the wall, but its shadow fell with marvellous distinctness upon the white panelling, and gave me the impression of someone crouching to waylay me. I stood rigid for half a minute perhaps. Then, with my hand in the pocket that held my revolver, I advanced, only to discover a Ganymede and Eagle glistening in the moonlight. That incident for a time restored my nerve, and a porcelain Chinaman on a buhl table, whose head rocked silently as I passed him, scarcely startled me.

The door to the red room and the steps up to it were in a shadowy corner. I moved my candle from side to side, in order to see clearly the nature of the recess in which I stood before opening the door. Here it was, thought I, that my predecessor was found, and the memory of that story gave me a sudden twinge of apprehension. I glanced over my shoulder at the Ganymede in the moonlight, and opened the door of the red room rather hastily, with my face half turned to the pallid silence of the landing.

I entered, closed the door behind me at once, turned the key I found in the lock within, and stood with the candle held aloft, surveying the scene of my vigil, the great red room of Lorraine Castle, in which the young duke had died. Or, rather, in which he had begun his dying, for he had opened the door and fallen headlong down the steps I had just ascended.

That had been the end of his vigil, of his gallant attempt to conquer the ghostly tradition of the place, and never, I thought, had apoplexy better served the ends of superstition. And there were other and older stories that clung to the room, back to the half-credible beginning of it all, the tale of a timid wife and the tragic end that came to her husband's jest of frightening her. And looking around that large sombre room, with its shadowy window bays, its recesses and alcoves, one could well understand the legends that had sprouted in its black corners, its germinating darkness. My candle was a little tongue of light in its vastness, that failed to pierce the opposite end of the room, and left an ocean of mystery and suggestion, sentinel shadows and watching darkness beyond its island of light. And the stillness of desolation brooded over it all.

I must confess some impalpable quality of that ancient room disturbed me. I tried to fight the feeling down. I resolved to make a systematic examination of the place at once, and dispel the fanciful suggestions of its obscurity before they obtained a hold upon me. After satisfying myself of the fastening of the door, I began to walk about the room, peering round each article of furniture, tucking up the valances of the bed, and opening its curtains wide. In one place there was a distinct echo to my footsteps, the noises I made seemed so little that they enhanced rather than broke the silence of the place. I pulled up the blinds and examined the fastenings of the several windows before closing the shutters, leant forward and looked up the blackness of the wide chimney, and tapped the dark oak panelling for any secret opening. There were two big mirrors in the room, each with a pair of sconces bearing candles, and on the mantelshelf, too, were more candles in china candlesticks. All these I lit one after the other.

The fire was laid, an unexpected consideration from the old housekeeper,—and I lit it, to keep down any disposition to shiver, and when it was burning well, I stood round with my back to it and regarded the room again. I had pulled up a chintz-covered armchair and a table, to form a kind of barricade before me, and on this lay my revolver ready to hand. My precise examination had done me good, but I still found the remote darkness of the place, and its perfect stillness, too stimulating for the imagination. The echoing of the stir and crackling of the fire was no sort of comfort to me. The shadow in the alcove at the end in particular, had that undefinable quality of a presence, that odd suggestion of a lurking, living thing, that comes so easily in silence and solitude. At last, to reassure myself, I walked with a candle into it, and satisfied myself that there was nothing tangible there. I stood that candle upon the floor of the alcove, and left it in that position.

By this time I was in a state of considerable nervous tension, although to my reason there was no adequate cause for the condition. My mind, however, was perfectly clear. I postulated quite unreservedly that nothing supernatural could happen, and to pass the time I began to string some rhymes together, Ingoldsby fashion, of the original legend of the place. A few I spoke aloud, but the echoes were not pleasant. For the same reason I also abandoned, after a time, a conversation with myself upon the impossibility of ghosts and haunting. My mind reverted to the three old and distorted people downstairs, and I tried to keep it upon that topic.

The sombre reds and blacks of the room troubled me; even with seven candles the place was merely dim. The one in the alcove flared in a draught, and the fire-flickering kept the shadows and penumbra perpetually shifting and stirring. Casting about for a remedy, I recalled the candles I had seen in the passage, and, with a slight effort, walked out into the moonlight, carrying a candle and leaving the door open, and presently returned with as many as ten. These I put in various knick-knacks of china with which the room was sparsely adorned, lit and placed where the shadows had lain deepest, some on the floor, some in the window recesses, until at last my seventeen candles were so arranged that not an inch of the room but had the direct light of at least one of them. It occurred to me that when the ghost came, I could warn him not to trip over them.

The room was now quite brightly illuminated. There was something very cheery and reassuring in these little streaming flames, and snuffing them gave me an occupation, and afforded a helpful sense of the passage of time. Even with that, however, the brooding expectation of the vigil weighed heavily upon me. It was after midnight that the candle in the alcove suddenly went out, and the black shadow sprang back to its place there. I did not see the candle go out; I simply turned and saw that the darkness was there, as one might start and see the unexpected presence of a stranger. 'By Jove!' said I aloud; 'that draught's a strong one!' and, taking the matches from the table, I walked across the room in a leisurely manner, to relight the corner again. My first match would not strike, and as I succeeded with the second, something seemed to blink on the wall before me. I turned my head involuntarily, and saw that the two candles on the little table by the fireplace were extinguished. I rose at once to my feet.

'Odd!' I said. 'Did I do that myself in a flash of absent-mindedness?'

I walked back, relit one, and as I did so, I saw the candle in the right sconce of one of the mirrors wink and go right out, and almost immediately its companion followed it. There was no mistake about it. The flame vanished, as if the wicks had been suddenly nipped between a finger and a thumb, leaving the wick neither glowing nor smoking, but black. While I stood gaping, the candle at the foot of the bed went out, and the shadows seemed to take another step towards me.

'This won't do!' said I, and first one and then another candle on the mantelshelf followed.

'What's up?' I cried, with a queer high note getting into my voice somehow. At that the candle on the wardrobe went out, and the one I had relit in the alcove followed.

'Steady on!' I said. 'These candles are wanted,' speaking with a half-hysterical facetiousness, and scratching away at a match the while for the mantel candlesticks. My hands trembled so much that twice I missed the rough paper of the matchbox. As the mantel emerged from darkness again, two candles in the remoter end of the window were eclipsed. But with the same match I also relit the larger mirror candles, and those on the floor near the doorway, so that for the moment I seemed to gain on the extinctions. But then in a volley there vanished four lights at once in different corners of the room, and I struck another match in quivering haste, and stood hesitating whither to take it.

As I stood undecided, an invisible hand seemed to sweep out the two candles on the table. With a cry of terror, I dashed at the alcove, then into the corner, and then into the window, relighting three, as two more vanished by the fireplace; then, perceiving a better way, I dropped the matches on the iron-bound deed-box in the corner, and caught up the bedroom candlestick. With this I avoided the delay of striking matches; but for all that the steady process of extinction went on, and the shadows I feared and fought against returned, and crept in upon me, first a step gained on this side of me and then on that. It was like a ragged storm-cloud sweeping out the stars. Now and then one returned for a minute, and was lost again. I was now almost frantic with the horror of the coming darkness, and my self-possession deserted me. I leaped panting and dishevelled from candle to candle, in a vain struggle against that remorseless advance.

I bruised myself on the thigh against the table, I sent a chair headlong, I stumbled and fell and whisked the cloth from the table in my fall. My candle rolled away from me, and I snatched another as I rose. Abruptly this was blown out, as I swung it off the table by the wind of my sudden movement, and immediately the two remaining candles followed. But there was light still in the room, a red light that staved off the shadows from me. The fire! Of course, I could still thrust my candle between the bars and relight it!

I turned to where the flames were still dancing between the glowing coals, and splashing red reflections upon the furniture, made two steps towards the grate, and incontinently the flames dwindled and vanished, the glow vanished, the reflections rushed together and vanished, and as I thrust the candle between the bars darkness closed upon me like the shutting of an eye, wrapped about me in a stifling embrace, sealed my vision, and crushed the last vestiges of reason from my brain. The candle fell from my hand. I flung out my arms in a vain effort to thrust that ponderous blackness away from me, and, lifting up my voice, screamed with all my might— once, twice, thrice. Then I think I must have staggered to my feet. I know I thought suddenly of the moonlit corridor, and, with my head bowed and my arms over my face, made a run for the door.

But I had forgotten the exact position of the door, and

struck myself heavily against the corner of the bed. I staggered back, turned, and was either struck or struck myself against some other bulky furniture. I have a vague memory of battering myself thus, to and fro in the darkness, of a cramped struggle, and of my own wild crying as I darted to and fro, of a heavy blow at last upon my forehead, a horrible sensation of falling that lasted an age, of my last frantic effort to keep my footing, and then I remember no more.

I opened my eyes in daylight. My head was roughly bandaged, and the man with the withered arm was watching my face. I looked about me, trying to remember what had happened, and for a space I could not recollect. I rolled my eyes into the corner, and saw the old woman, no longer abstracted, pouring out some drops of medicine from a little blue phial into a glass. 'Where am I?' I asked; 'I seem to remember you, and yet I cannot remember who you are.'

They told me then, and I heard of the haunted Red Room as one who hears a tale. 'We found you at dawn,' said he, 'and there was blood on your forehead and lips.'

It was very slowly I recovered my memory of my experience. 'You believe now,' said the old man, 'that the room is haunted?' He spoke no longer as one who greets an intruder, but as one who grieves for a broken friend.

'Yes,' said I; 'the room is haunted.'

'And you have seen it. And we, who have lived here all our lives, have never set eyes upon it. Because we have never dared. Tell us, is it truly the old earl who——'

'No,' said I; 'it is not.'

'I told you so,' said the old lady, with the glass in her

hand. 'It is his poor young countess who was frightened—'

'It is not,' I said. 'There is neither ghost of an earl nor ghost of a countess in that room, there is no ghost there at all; but worse, far worse——'

'Well?' they said.

'The worst of all the things that haunt poor mortal men,' said I; 'and that is, in all its nakedness—Fear that will not have light nor sound, that will not bear with reason, that deafens and darkens and overwhelms. It followed me through the corridor, it fought against me in the room—'

I stopped abruptly. There was an interval of silence. My hand went up to my bandages.

Then the man with the shade sighed and spoke. 'That is it,' said he. 'I knew that was it. A power of darkness. To put such a curse upon a woman! It lurks there always. You can feel it even in the daytime, even of a bright summer's day, in the hangings, in the curtains, keeping behind you however you face about. In the dusk it creeps along the corridor and follows you, so that you dare not turn. There is Fear in that room of hers—black Fear, and there will be—so long as this house of sin endures.'

Brother Rabbit's Cradle

Joel Chandler Harris

'I wish you'd tell me what you tote a hankcher fer,' remarked Uncle Remus, after he had reflected over the matter a little while.

'Why, to keep my mouth clean,' answered the little boy. Uncle Remus looked at the lad, and shook his head doubtfully. 'Uh-uh!' he exclaimed. 'You can't fool folks when dey git ez ol' ez what I is. I been watchin' you now mo' days dan I kin count, an' I ain't never see yo' mouf dirty 'nuff fer ter be wiped wid a hankcher. It's allers clean—too clean fer ter suit me. Dar's yo' pa, now; when he wuz a little chap like you, his mouf useter git dirty in de mornin' an' stay dirty plum twel night. Dey wa'n't sca'cely a day dat he didn't look like he been playin' wid de pigs in de stable lot. Ef he yever is tote a hankcher, he ain't never show it ter me.'

'He carries one now,' remarked the little boy with something like a triumphant look on his face.

'Tooby sho', said Uncle Remus; 'tooby sho' he do. He start ter totin' one when he tuck an' tuck a notion fer ter go a-courtin'. It had his name in one cornder, an' he useter sprinkle it wid stuff out'n a pepper-sauce bottle. It sho' wuz rank, dat stuff wuz; it smell so sweet it make you fergit whar you live at. I take notice dat you ain't got none on yone.'

'No; mother says that cologne or any kind of perfumery on your handkerchief makes you common.'

Uncle Remus leaned his head back, closed his eyes, and permitted a heart-rending groan to issue from his lips. The little boy showed enough anxiety to ask him what the matter was. 'Nothin' much, honey; I wuz des tryin' fer ter count how many diffunt kinder people dey is in dis big worl', an' 'fo' I got mo' dan half done wid my countin', a pain struck me in my mizry, an' I had ter break off.'

'I know what you mean,' said the child. 'You think mother is queer; grandmother thinks so too.'

'How come you to be so wise, honey?' Uncle Remus inquired, opening his eyes wide with astonishment.

'I know by the way you talk, and by the way grandmother looks sometimes,' answered the little boy.

Uncle Remus said nothing for some time. When he did speak, it was to lead the little boy to believe that he had been all the time engaged in thinking about something else. 'Talkin' er dirty folks,' he said, 'you oughter seed yo' pa when he wuz a little bit er chap. Dey wuz long days when you couldn't tell ef he wuz black er white, he wuz dat dirty. He'd come out'n de big house in de mornin' ez clean ez a new pin, an' 'fo' ten er-clock you couldn't tell what kinder clof his cloze wuz made out'n. Many's de day when I've seed ol' Miss—dat's yo' great-gran'mammy—comb 'nuff trash out'n his head fer ter fill a basket.'

The little boy laughed at the picture that Uncle Remus drew of his father. 'He's very clean, now,' said the lad loyally.

'Maybe he is an' maybe he ain't,' remarked Uncle Remus, suggesting a doubt. 'Dat's needer here ner dar. Is he any better off clean dan what he wuz when you couldn't put yo' han's on 'im widout havin' ter go an' wash um? Yo' gran'mammy useter call 'im a pig, an' clean ez he may be now, I take notice dat he makes mo' complaint er headache an' de heartburn dan what he done when he wuz runnin' roun' here half-naked an' full er mud. I hear tell dat some nights he can't git no sleep, but when he wuz little like you—no, suh, I'll not say dat, bekaze he wuz bigger dan what you is fum de time he kin toddle roun' widout nobody he'pin' him; but when he wuz ol' ez you an' twice ez big, dey ain't narry night dat he can't sleep—an' not only all night, but half de day ef dey'd 'a' let 'im. Ef dey'd let you run roun' here like he done, an' git dirty, you'd git big an' strong 'fo' you know it. Dey ain't nothin' mo' wholesomer dan a peck er two er clean dirt on a little chap like you.'

There is no telling what comment the child would have made on this sincere tribute to clean dirt, for his attention was suddenly attracted to something that was gradually taking shape in the hands of Uncle Remus. At first it seemed to be hardly worthy of notice, for it had been only a thin piece of board. But now the one piece had become four pieces, two long and two short, and under the deft manipulations of Uncle Remus it soon assumed a boxlike shape.

The old man had reached the point in his work where silence was necessary to enable him to do it full justice. As he fitted the thin boards together, a whistling sound issued from his lips, as though he were letting off steam; but the singular noise was due to the fact that he was completely absorbed in his work. He continued to fit and trim, and trim and fit, until finally the little boy could no longer restrain his curiosity. 'Uncle Remus, what are you making?' he asked plaintively.

'Larroes fer ter kech meddlers,' was the prompt and blunt reply.

'Well, what are larroes to catch meddlers?' the child insisted.

'Nothin' much an' sump'n mo'. Dicky, Dicky, killt a chicky, an' fried it quicky, in de oven, like a sloven. Den ter his daddy's Sunday hat, he tuck 'n' hitched de ol' black cat. Now what you reckon make him do dat? Ef you can't tell me word fer word an' spellin' fer spellin' we'll go out an' come in an' take a walk.'

He rose, grunting as he did so, thus paying an unintentional tribute to the efficacy of age as the partner of rheumatic aches and stiff joints. 'You hear me gruntin',' he remarked—'well, dat's bekaze I ain't de chicky fried by Dicky, which he e't 'nuff fer ter make 'im sicky.' As he went out the child took his hand, and went trotting along by his side, thus affording an interesting study for those who concern themselves with the extremes of life. Hand in hand the two went out into the fields, and thence into the great woods, where Uncle Remus, after searching about for some time, carefully deposited his oblong box, remarking: 'Ef I don't make no mistakes, dis ain't so mighty fur fum de place whar de creeturs has der playgroun', an' dey ain't no tellin' but what one un um'll creep in dar when deyer playin' hidin', an' ef he do, he'll sho be our meat.'

'Oh, it's a trap!' exclaimed the little boy, his face lighting up with enthusiasm.

'An' dey wa'n't nobody here ter tell you,' Uncle Remus declared, astonishment in his tone. 'Well, ef dat don't bang my time, I ain't no free nigger. Now, ef dat had 'a' been yo' pa at de same age, I'd 'a' had ter tell 'im forty-lev'm times, an' den he wouldn't 'a' b'lieved me twel he see sump'n in dar tryin' fer ter git out. Den he'd say it wuz a trap, but not befo'. I ain't blamin' 'im,' Uncle Remus went on, 'kaze 'tain't eve'y chap dat kin tell a trap time he see it, an' mo' dan dat, traps don' allers sketch what dey er sot fer.'

He paused, looked all around, and up in the sky, where fleecy clouds were floating lazily along, and in the tops of the trees, where the foliage was swaying gently in the breeze. Then he looked at the little boy. 'Ef I ain't gone an' got los,' he said, 'we ain't so mighty fur fum de place whar Mr Man, once 'pon a time—not yo' time ner yit my time, but some time—tuck'n' sot a trap for Brer Rabbit. In dem days, dey hadn't l'arnt how ter be kyarpenters, an' dish yer trap what I'm tellin' you 'bout wuz a great big contraption. Big ez Brer Rabbit wuz, it wuz lots too big fer him.'

'Now, whiles Mr Man wuz fixin' up dis trap, Mr Rabbit wa'n't so mighty fur off. He hear de saw—er-rash! er-rash!— an' he hear de hammer—bang, bang, bang!—an' he ax hisse'f what all dis racket wuz 'bout. He see Mr Man come out'n his yard totin' sump'n, an' he got furder off; he see Mr Man comin' todes de bushes, an' he tuck ter de woods; he see 'im

comin' todes de woods, an' he tuck ter de bushes. Mr Man
tote de trap so fur an' no furder. He put it down, he did, an'
Brer Rabbit watch 'im; he put in de bait, an' Brer Rabbit
watch 'im; he fix de trigger, an' still Brer Rabbit watch 'im.
Mr Man look at de trap an' it satchify him. He look at it an'
laugh, an' when he do dat, Brer Rabbit wunk one eye, an'
wiggle his mustache, an' chaw his cud.

'An' dat ain't all he do, needer. He sot out in de bushes,
he did, an' study how ter git some game in de trap. He study
so hard, an' he got so errytated, dat he thumped his behime
foot on de groun' twel it soun' like a cow dancin' out dar
in de bushes, but 'twan't no cow, ner yit no calf—'twuz des
Brer Rabbit studyin'. Atter so long a time, he put out down
de road todes dat part er de country whar mos' er de creeturs
live at. Eve'y time he hear a fuss, he'd dodge in de bushes,
kaze he wanter see who comin'. He keep on an' he keep on,
an' bimeby he hear ol' Brer Wolf trottin' down de road.

'It so happen dat Brer Wolf wuz de ve'y one what Brer
Rabbit wanter see. Dey wuz perlit ter one an'er, but dey wan't
no frien'ly feelin' 'twix um. Well, here come ol' Brer Wolf,
hongrier dan a chicken-hawk on a frosty mornin', an' ez he
come up he see Brer Rabbit set by de side er de road lookin'
like he done lose all his fambly an' his friends terboot.'

'Dey pass de time er day, an' den Brer Wolf kinder grin
an' say, 'Laws-a-massy, Brer Rabbit! What ail you? You look
like you done had a spell er fever an' ague; what de trouble?'
'Trouble, Brer Wolf? You ain't never see no trouble twel you
git whar I'm at. Maybe you wouldn't min' it like I does, kaze I
ain't usen ter it. But I boun' you done seed me light-minded

fer de las' time. I'm done—I'm plum wo' out,' sez Brer Rabbit, sezee. Dis make Brer Wolf open his eyes wide. He say, 'Dis de fus' time I ever is hear you talk dat-a-way, Brer Rabbit; take yo' time an' tell me 'bout it. I ain't had my brekkus yit, but dat don't make no diffunce, long ez youer in trouble. I'll he'p you out ef I kin, an' mo' dan dat, I'll put some heart in de work.' When he say dis, he grin an' show his tushes, an' Brer Rabbit kinder edge 'way fum 'im. He say, 'Tell me de trouble, Brer Rabbit, an' I'll do my level bes' fer ter he'p you out.'

'Wid dat, Brer Rabbit 'low dat Mr Man done been had 'im hired fer ter take keer er his truck patch, an' keep out de minks, de mush-rats an' de weasels. He say dat he done so well settin' up night atter night, when he des might ez well been in bed, dat Mr Man prommus 'im sump'n extry 'sides de mess er greens what he gun 'im eve'y day. Atter so long a time, he say, Mr Man 'low dat he gwineter make 'im a present uv a cradle so he kin rock de little Rabs ter sleep when dey cry. So said, so done, he say. Mr Man make de cradle an' tell Brer Rabbit he kin take it home wid 'im.'

'He start out wid it, he say, but it got so heavy he hatter set it down in de woods, an' dat's de reason why Brer Wolf seed 'im settin' down by de side er de road, lookin' like he in deep trouble. Brer Wolf sot down, he did, an' study, an' bimeby he say he'd like mighty well fer ter have a cradle fer his chillun, long ez cradles wuz de style. Brer Rabbit say dey been de style fer de longest, an' ez fer Brer Wolf wantin' one, he say he kin have de one what Mr Man make fer him, kaze it's lots too big fer his chillun. 'You know how folks is,' sez Brer Rabbit, sezee. 'Dey try ter do what dey dunner how ter do, an' dar's der house bigger dan a barn, an' dar's de fence wid mo' holes in it dan what dey is in a saine, an' kaze dey have great big chillun dey got de idee dat eve'y cradle what dey make mus' fit der own chillun. An' dat's how come I can't tote de cradle what Mr Man make fer me mo' dan ten steps at a time.'

'Brer Wolf ax Brer Rabbit what he gwineter do fer a cradle, an' Brer Rabbit 'low he kin manage fer ter git 'long wid de ol' one twel he kin 'suade Mr Man ter make 'im an'er one, an' he don't speck dat'll be so mighty hard ter do. Brer Wolf can't he'p but b'lieve dey's some trick in it, an' he say he ain't see de ol' cradle when las' he wuz at Brer Rabbit house. Wid dat, Brer Rabbit bust out laughin'. He say, 'Dat's been so long back, Brer Wolf, dat I done fergit all 'bout it; 'sides dat, ef dey wuz a cradle dar, I boun' you my ol' 'oman got better sense dan ter set de cradle in der parler, whar comp'ny comes'; an' he laugh so loud an' long dat he make Brer Wolf right shame er himse'f.

'He 'low, ol' Brer Wolf did, 'Come on, Brer Rabbit, an' show me whar de cradle is. Ef it's too big fer yo' chillun, it'll des 'bout fit mine.' An' so off dey put ter whar Mr Man done sot his trap. 'Twa'n't so mighty long 'fo' dey got whar dey wuz gwine, an' Brer Rabbit say, 'Brer Wolf, dar yo' cradle, an' may it do you mo' good dan it's yever done me!' Brer Wolf walk all roun' de trap an' look at it like 'twuz live. Brer Rabbit thump one er his behime foots on de groun' an' Brer Wolf jump like some un done shot a gun right at 'im. Dis make Brer Rabbit laugh twel he can't laugh no mo'. Brer Wolf, he say he kinder nervous 'bout dat time er de year, an' de leas' little bit er noise 'll make 'im jump. He ax how he gwineter git any purchis on de cradle, an' Brer Rabbit say he'll hatter git inside an' walk wid it on his back, kaze dat de way he done done.

'Brer Wolf ax what all dem contraptions on de inside is, an' Brer Rabbit 'spon' dat dey er de rockers, an' dey ain't no needs fer ter be skeer'd un um, kaze dey ain't nothin' but plain wood. Brer Wolf say he ain't 'zactly skeer'd, but he done got ter de p'int whar he know dat you better look 'fo' you jump. Brer Rabbit 'low dat ef dey's any jumpin' fer ter be done, he de one ter do it, an' he talk like he done fergit what dey come fer. Brer Wolf, he fool an' fumble roun', but bimeby he walk in de cradle, sprung de trigger, an' dar he wuz! Brer Rabbit, he holler out, 'Come on, Brer Wolf; des hump yo'se'f, an' I'll be wid you.' But try ez he will an' grunt ez he may, Brer Wolf can't budge dat trap. Bimeby Brer Rabbit git tired er waitin', an' he say dat ef Brer Wolf ain't gwineter come on he's gwine home. He 'low dat a frien' what say he gwineter he'p you, an' den go in a cradle an' drap off ter sleep, dat's all he wanter know 'bout um; an' wid dat he made fer de bushes, an' he wa'n't a minnit too soon, kaze here come Mr Man fer ter see ef his trap had been sprung. He look, he did, an', sho 'nuff, it 'uz sprung, an' dey wuz sump'n in dar, too, kaze he kin hear it rustlin' roun' an' kickin' fer ter git out.

'Mr Man look thoo de crack, an' he see Brer Wolf, which he wuz so skeer'd twel his eye look right green. Mr Man say, 'Aha! I got you, is I?' Brer Wolf say, 'Who?' Mr Man laugh twel he can't sca'cely talk, an' still Brer Wolf say, 'Who? Who you think you got?' Mr Man say, 'low, 'I don't think, I knows. Youer ol' Brer Rabbit, dat's who you is.' Brer Wolf say, 'Turn me outer here, an' I'll show you who I is.' Mr Man laugh fit ter kill. He say, 'low, 'You neenter change yo' voice; I'd know you ef I met you in de dark. Youer Brer Rabbit, dat's who you is.' Brer Wolf say, 'I ain't not; dat's what I'm not!'

'Mr Man look thoo de crack ag'in, an' he see de short ears. He 'low, 'You done cut off yo' long ears, but still I knows you. Oh, yes! an' you done sharpen yo' mouf an' put smut on it—but you can't fool me.' Brer Wolf say, 'Nobody ain't tryin' fer ter fool you. Look at my fine long bushy tail.' Mr Man say, 'low, 'You done tied an'er tail on behime you, but you can't fool me. Oh, no, Brer Rabbit! You can't fool me.' Brer Wolf say, 'Look at de ha'r on my back; do dat look like Brer Rabbit?' Mr Man say, 'low, 'You done wallered in de red san', but you can't fool me.'

'Brer Wolf say, 'Look at my long black legs; do dey look like Brer Rabbit?' Mr Man 'low, 'You kin put an'er j'int in yo' legs, an' you kin smut um, but you can't fool me.' Brer Wolf say, 'Look at my tushes; does dey look like Brer Rabbit?' Mr Man 'low, 'You done got your toofies, but you can't fool me.' Brer Wolf say, 'Look at my little eyes; does dey look like Brer Rabbit?' Mr Man 'low, 'You kin squinch yo' eye-balls, but you can't fool me, Brer Rabbit.' Brer Wolf squall out, 'I ain't not Brer Rabbit, an' yo' better turn me out er dis place so I kin take hide an' ha'r off'n Brer Rabbit.' Mr Man say, 'Ef bofe hide an' ha'r wuz off, I'd know you, kaze 'tain't in you fer ter fool me.' An' it hurt Brer Wolf feelin's so bad fer Mr Man ter sput his word, dat he bust out inter a big boo-boo, an' dat's 'bout all I know.'

'Did the man really and truly think that Brother Wolf was

Brother Rabbit?' asked the little boy.

'When you pin me dawn dat-a-way,' responded Uncle Remus, 'I'm bleeze ter tell you dat I ain't too certain an' sho' 'bout dat. De tale come down fum my great-gran'daddy's great-gran'daddy; it come on down ter my daddy, an' des ez he gun it ter me, des dat-a-way I done gun it ter you.'

The Last Ticket

Minoo Karimzadeh

THE LINE at the bus stop was getting longer, but there was no sign of the bus. Sohrab stepped up to stand behind the last person at the end of the line. The old man standing in front of him asked, 'It's seven o'clock, isn't it?'

Sohrab glanced at the sky and said, 'I guess so.'

Farther up the line was a youngster holding some textbooks in his hand. Sohrab gazed at the books, trying to read the title of one of them from where he was standing, and with difficulty he read, 'Natural Sciences.' Then the sounds of school bell, hammer strokes and stone cutting machine mingled in his mind. He shook his head as if to get rid of those sounds.

The bus passed them and stopped at the head of the line. The crowd moved. Sohrab reached into his breast pocket, felt two tickets, took one out and shuffled forward with the line. Inside the bus he sat on the last seat next to the window, and the old man sat beside him. Soon the bus filled with passengers. Sohrab crossed his arms, put them over his chest, lowered himself on the seat and pressed his knees to the back of the seat in front of him. He leaned his head against the window and was about to close his black and sleepy eyes when the old man asked, 'Where do you get off?'

'At the last stop.'

'So that's why you're trying to make yourself so comfortable.'

Sohrab laughed. The heat inside the bus made him drowsy. He closed his eyes, and soon was far from hearing anything.

Sohrab got off, and went all the way down the alley. Reaching the last house, he took a small set of keys out of his pocket, opened the door, and slowly climbed up the stairs. When he got to the second floor he saw his mother cleaning the glass globe of the oil lamp. He moved forward and, untying his shoelaces said,

'Hello.'

'Hello, Sonny. Hope you're not tired.'

'How's Soodabeh?'

'Thank God, she's better. Mehri Khanoom gave me some quince seeds to give her, and now she wheezes less and breathes more easily.'

Sohrab opened the door of the room, and the heat struck his face. Soodabeh was sleeping in her bed in the corner of the room. Sohrab went near the stove, picked up the kettle and held his hands over the stove. His mother came into the room. She put the pot on the stove and said, 'Khosro should be here any minute.' Then she turned to Sohrab and asked,

'What's the date today?'

'It's the 28th.'

'This month we really had difficulty in making ends meet. I don't have even one rial[1] left in my purse. When will you get paid?'

'The day after tomorrow.'

'Isn't it possible for you to get two months' pay in advance? Khosro says he has heard news from the village that Aziz is ill in bed and she has no money. The old woman has nobody except us.'

'Mom, what are you talking about? The boss doesn't even pay one day's wage in advance, and you think he may give me a month's pay in advance?'

Then, as if recalling something, he turned to his mother and said, 'By the way, why don't we get Aziz to come and stay with us?'

His mother got up and walked over to sit on the bed beside Soodabeh. As she gently shook her daughter to wake her, she said, 'My dear son, we are not properly settled in this polluted city ourselves. What's the good of asking Aziz to come here? Anyhow, Khosro has already told her several times to do so, but she has replied, "You should come back and stay with me. I'm all right. You are the ones who are separated from your roots".'

The wail of a fire engine siren could be heard from the street. Sohrab's mother listened to it briefly, then got up, and as if talking to herself, said, 'Mind you, she's not wrong. We

---

[1]The basic monetary unit of Iran.

have always been wondering, and now even more than ever. We are like beheaded birds in this big city where we have to flutter our wings until we die.'

From the stairs they could hear Khosro talking to the landlady. Sohrab's mother got to her feet, went to the door and, turning to Sohrab, said in a low voice, 'What do you know? Maybe after all we will go back since Khosro is also very discouraged.'

In the morning, Sohrab opened the door of the house and stepped outside. The alley was covered in snow and the day was breaking. He glanced at the sky, put his hands into his pockets and started off. The fresh snow crunched under his feet. As he reached the square he looked at the bus stop. Empty buses were picking passengers up and leaving. Sohrab reached into his breast pocket and remembered he had only one ticket left. He looked at the bus stop again, wondering what he was going to do at night. Then he started off walking. 'It's better to go on foot now; at night I'll be dead tired and it'll be more difficult.'

The snow-covered ground forced him to slow down. After a few feet he turned back and had a glance at the bus stop, 'If I continue walking at this slow pace, I won't get there even by noon.'

He headed back to the bus stop, and again reached into his breast pocket. In a short while, he was in the line moving forward slowly. He thought of his return trip at night and was about to get out of the line when, unbidden, a question came to his mind, 'Is it possible to get on the bus without a ticket?'

The man in front of him suddenly turned around, looked

at him, and without saying a word again turned his head. Sohrab grew pale at once, thinking, 'He must have realized.' He lowered his head and felt his knees tremble. The sounds of hammer strokes and a stonecutting machine echoed in his ears. The line beside the bus looked like a fallen tree with its branches near the door. The people were pushing their way onto the bus, and before Sohrab knew it, he was standing in the aisle. Then he froze as he heard the driver cry out, 'Hey you, where's your ticket?'

Sohrab's legs felt weak and his knees trembled. He was putting his hand into his pocket when he heard someone say, 'You're talking to me?'

'Who else do you think I'm talking to? Hurry up.'

Sohrab looked at the person talking to the driver. He was a middle-aged man in a black coat, high plastic boots and a new hat, and was firmly holding the hand of a four or five-year-old child.

The man patted the child's hair and said, 'What are you talking about?'

'Ticket. Your ticket.'

'How many times should I give my ticket?'

'Give it to me just once and keep the rest for yourself.'

'I gave you my ticket.'

The driver shouted, 'So you did!'

'Yes.'

'Do you mean to tell me that there's something wrong with my eyes at this early hour?'

'That I don't know, but I did give my ticket; otherwise, how did I get on the bus?'

'Now, here we go again! Come off it Mister! I don't want the ticket for myself.'

The man didn't answer. He turned his face to look outside and muttered something to himself.

The driver started the bus and cautiously pulled away on the slippery snow out of the bus stop. Then farther down he pulled over. He pulled up the handbrake and turned the motor off.

One of the passengers said sarcastically, 'This is all we need.'

The driver, scanning the inside of the bus through his rear-view mirror, calmly said, 'We aren't going to move unless you give me your ticket.'

The man said, 'What trouble I've gotten into because of this guy!'

A well-groomed young man in a brown leather jacket turned to the man and said, 'All this fuss over one ticket. Surrender the ticket and let's get through with all this.'

The man replied sharply, 'What do you mean by "let's get through with it?" I said I've given my ticket, and I'm not giving another one.'

The man standing next to Sohrab looked at him and said, 'You see how people disgrace themselves just for one *toman.*'

The man's face turned red and he shouted, 'You speak as if I'm a thief!'

Sohrab suddenly got scared and looked down.

'Surely he knows I'm the one who hasn't given his ticket.'

The driver bent down, passed below the bar and went into the aisle. He grabbed the man's collar and said, 'You're really trying my patience. Either you give your ticket or you get off right away.'

A passenger said, 'Have mercy on the poor child trembling with fear.'

The boy was holding fast to the man's coat and with terrified eyes was staring at the driver.

The man, his forehead now covered with perspiration, brought up his hands, pushed the driver away, grabbed the boy's hand and said, 'I'm not as helpless as you think. I'll go and complain to the person in charge of this line.'

The driver pointed to the door and said, 'Good idea! Let's go.'

Following the man out, the driver said, 'What a life! You can't even state what is right.'

Passengers watched through the windows as the driver, the man and the boy walked down the street and went into the office. From their angry gestures it was obvious that they were having a fight. Some passengers grumbled and got off the bus.

Staring at the office, one passenger said, 'Some people don't even care to know whom they are cheating.'

A man wearing a black shirt and sitting on the seat next to which Sohrab was standing said, 'Maybe he succeeds in cheating here and now. What is he going to do in the next world?'

Sohrab felt the man was staring at him while speaking these words. He thought everyone was now staring at him. He didn't dare to look up. His legs had become like two dry sticks and he couldn't feel them.

A woman said, 'You all speak as if he has killed someone. He just hasn't given his ticket. That's all. Maybe he couldn't afford one. Was it necessary to make all this fuss?'

Sohrab took heart at this and raised his head a little to see the woman, but heard someone else say, 'There's no way you can justify theft. These guys are thieves.'

Blood rushed to Sohrab's face. He was thinking that if he were to raise his head everyone would look at him, and probably someone would even cry out, 'Thief!'

The uproar in the bus was slowly subsiding. Passengers became silent. Sohrab thought they were silent because they were on the watch to prevent him from escaping. He was scared of everyone. 'I wish I had gone on foot. I shouldn't have worried about being late or being scolded.'

Suddenly, a voice interrupted his thoughts, 'There he comes.'

Everyone turned towards the windows. The driver was walking towards the bus. The man and the boy were still in the office. The driver got on the bus and angrily muttered to himself, 'Damned people. They think I want the ticket for myself.'

He sat behind the wheel, released the handbrake, looked at the side mirror and slowly drove off.

Sohrab suddenly moved. Hesitantly and with fear he started walking and in a high voice, though he intended it to be low, he said, 'Stop.'

The driver hesitated and looked into the mirror, 'You want me to stop?'

'Yes sir, I've made a mistake.'

'What mistake? There's only one bus line here.'

Sohrab insisted, 'But I've made a mistake and I want to get off.'

The driver braked suddenly, opened the door and said, 'My goodness! What's going on today? One wants to get on by force and another wants to get off by force.'

Sohrab hurriedly went towards the door, afraid to hear someone shout, 'Don't let him escape!' But, except for an old man's voice who was grumbling because he had stepped on his foot, he heard nothing. After he got off he was hesitant to look at the bus, but finally turned and looked. Some passengers had wiped the steam from the windows and Sohrab could see their drowsy eyes. Not a single one was looking at him.

Sohrab breathed deeply. He clapped his hands with joy and watched his crowded prison moving away. Thank God! He roared with laughter and started off. He still had half the way to walk.

The night sky was clear, the stars so bright that it seemed one could reach out and pluck them. The trampled snow on the pavement had become slushy, and was now beginning to freeze. The gust of icy air which struck his face was so cold that he felt as though his skin would split open.

The streets were deserted, and Sohrab guessed it was about eight o'clock. He was hunched down walking towards the bus stop. When he opened his coat to take out the ticket, the cold penetrated his body and he trembled all over. He took out the ticket and thrust both hands into his coat pockets. The frozen water on the pavement crunched beneath his steps. There was nobody at the bus stop. The empty bus was parked a few feet away, and Sohrab gazed at it for a while.

'So much the better that the boss didn't let me leave earlier. He wanted me to make up for the morning. The bus is empty now and the streets are deserted; I'll get home in no time.' Then he yawned. His breath turned to mist, formed a white cloud and floated up in front of his eyes. He sat on the curb beside the gutter and put his head between his knees to warm his ears. After a short while he felt someone sit down beside him. He looked up. It was a boy almost his size, maybe a little smaller. He was wearing a raincoat and green cotton trousers with oil spots on them.

The boy glanced at Sohrab and said, 'Hope you're not tired.'

Sohrab replied, 'You, too.' Then he asked, 'Are you a mechanic?'

'Yes.'

'You've been working till now?'

'If you leave it up to my boss, he'll make you work until midnight.'

A bus that was passing the street on the other side attracted the boy's attention. As if remembering something he reached into his pocket and then got up, searched his trousers pockets and said to Sohrab, 'Do you have an extra ticket?'

Sohrab hesitantly said, 'An extra ticket!'

Then he stared at the boy's tired eyes. He took his hand out of his pocket and held out the ticket. The boy took it and put his hands in his trousers' pockets again. He bent his knees a little as if it would help him reach the bottom of his pocket, and then did the same with the other pocket.

Sohrab touched the boy's arm, and while the boy's hand was still in his pocket, said 'I don't want money for it.'

'But...'

'There's no "but."'

'But it's not possible...'

'I said I don't want money.'

The boy finally accepted. He looked at Sohrab with eyes full of gratitude and said, 'Thank you.'

Sohrab grabbed the boy's arm and pulled him aside. The bus stood in front of them. Sohrab stepped aside and told the boy, 'Get on.'

The boy asked in surprise, 'Aren't you getting on?'

'No. I have to take another bus.'

The boy got on the bus, and in the same surprised tone said, 'Goodbye.'

The bus with its streamed up windows passed in front of Sohrab. He stood and looked at the bus taking the boy away for a while. Then he stepped onto the pavement, put his hands in his pockets, stamped his feet a few times, and started off.

Translated by Shirin Nayer-Noori

The Red-Headed League

Arthur Conan Doyle

I HAD CALLED upon my friend, Mr Sherlock Holmes, one day in the autumn of last year, and found him in deep conversation with a very stout, florid-faced elderly gentleman, with fiery red hair. With an apology for my intrusion, I was about to withdraw, when Holmes pulled me abruptly into the room and closed the door behind me.

'You could not possibly have come at a better time, my dear Watson,' he said, cordially.

'I was afraid that you were engaged.'

'So I am. Very much so.'

'Then I can wait in the next room.'

'Not at all. This gentleman, Mr Wilson, has been my partner and helper in many of my most successful cases, and I have no doubt that he will be of the utmost use to me in yours also.'

The stout gentleman half rose from his chair and gave a

bob of greeting, with a quick little questioning glance from his small, fat-encircled eyes.

'Try the settee,' said Holmes, relapsing into his armchair, and putting his finger tips together, as was his custom when in judicial moods. 'I know, my dear Watson, that you share my love of all that is bizarre and outside the conventions and humdrum routine of everyday life. You have shown your relish for it by the enthusiasm which has prompted you to chronicle, and, if you will excuse my saying so, somewhat to embellish so many of my own little adventures.'

'Your cases have indeed been of the greatest interest to me,' I observed.

'You will remember that I remarked the other day, just before we went into the very simple problem presented by Miss Mary Sutherland, that for strange effects and extraordinary combinations we must go to life itself, which is always far more daring than any effort of the imagination.'

'A proposition which I took the liberty of doubting.'

'You did, doctor, but none the less you must come round to my view, for otherwise I shall keep on piling fact upon fact on you, until your reason breaks down under them and acknowledge me to be right. Now, Mr Jabez Wilson here has been good enough to call upon me this morning, and to begin a narrative which promises to be one of the most singular which I have listened to for some time. You have heard me remark that the strangest and most unique things are very often connected not with the larger but with the smaller crimes, and occasionally, indeed, where there is room for doubt whether any positive crime has been committed. As far as I have heard, it is impossible for me to say whether the present case is an instance of crime or not, but the course of events is certainly among the most singular that I have ever listened to. Perhaps, Mr Wilson, you would have the great kindness to recommence your narrative. I ask you, not merely because my friend, Dr Watson, has not heard the opening part, but also because the peculiar nature of the story makes me anxious to have every possible detail from your lips. As a rule, when I have heard some slight indication of the course of events I am able to guide myself by the thousands of other similar cases which occur to my memory. In the present instance I am forced to admit that the facts are, to the best of my belief, unique.'

The portly client puffed out his chest with an appearance of some little pride, and pulled a dirty and wrinkled newspaper from the inside pocket of his greatcoat. As he glanced down the advertisement column, with his head thrust forward, and the paper flattened out upon his knee, I took a good look at the man, and endeavoured, after the fashion of my companion, to read the indications which might be presented by his dress or appearance.

I did not gain very much, however, by my inspection. Our visitor bore every mark of being an average commonplace British tradesman, obese, pompous, and slow. He wore rather baggy grey shepherd's check trousers, a not over-clean black frock coat, unbuttoned in the front, and a drab waistcoat with a heavy brassy Albert chain, and a square pierced bit of metal dangling down as an ornament. A frayed top hat and a faded brown overcoat with a wrinkled velvet collar lay upon a chair beside him. Altogether, look as I would, there was nothing remarkable about the man save his blazing red head and the expression of extreme chagrin and discontent upon his features.

Sherlock Holmes's quick eye took in my occupation, and he shook his head with a smile as he noticed my questioning glances. 'Beyond the obvious facts that he has at some time done manual labour, that he takes snuff, that he is a Freemason, that he has been to China, and that he has done a considerable amount of writing lately, I can deduce nothing else.'

Mr Jabez Wilson started up in his chair, with his forefinger upon the paper, but his eyes upon my companion.

'How, in the name of good fortune, did you know all that, Mr Holmes?' he asked. 'How did you know, for example, that I did manual labour? It's as true as gospel, for I began as a ship's carpenter.'

'Your hands, my dear sir. Your right hand is quite a size larger than your left. You have worked with it and the muscles are more developed.'

'Well, the snuff, then, and the Freemasonry?'

'I won't insult your intelligence by telling you how I read that, especially as, rather against the strict rules of your order, you use an arc and compass breastpin.'

'Ah, of course, I forgot that. But the writing?'

'What else can be indicated by that right cuff so very shiny for five inches, and the left one with the smooth patch near the elbow where you rest it upon the desk.'

'Well, but China?'

'The fish which you have tattooed immediately above your wrist could only have been done in China. I have made a small study of tattoo marks, and have even contributed to the literature of the subject. That trick of staining the fishes' scales of a delicate pink is quite peculiar to China. When, in addition, I see a Chinese coin hanging from your watch chain, the matter becomes even more simple.'

Mr Jabez Wilson laughed heavily. 'Well, I never!' said he. 'I thought at first that you had done something clever, but I see that there was nothing in it after all.'

'I begin to think, Watson,' said Holmes, 'that I make a mistake in explaining. 'Omne ignotom pro magnifico,' you know, and my poor little reputation, such as it is, will suffer shipwreck if I am so candid. Can you not find the advertisement, Mr Wilson?'

'Yes, I have got it now,' he answered, with his thick, red finger planted halfway down the column. 'Here it is. This is what began it all. You just read it for yourself, sir.'

I took the paper from him and read as follows:

'TO THE RED-HEADED LEAGUE: On account of the bequest of the late Ezekiah Hopkins, of Lebanon, Pa., U.S.A., there is now another vacancy open which entitles a member of the League to a salary of four pounds a week for purely nominal services. All red-headed men who are sound in body and mind and above the age of twenty-one years are eligible. Apply in person on Monday, at eleven o'clock, to Duncan Ross, at the offices of the League, 7 Pope's Court, Fleet Street.'

'What on earth does this mean?' I ejaculated, after I had twice read over the extraordinary announcement.

Holmes chuckled and wriggled in his chair, as was his habit when in high spirits. 'It is a little off the beaten track, isn't it?' said he. 'And now, Mr Wilson, off you go at scratch, and tell us all about yourself, your household, and the effect which this advertisement had upon your fortunes. You will first make a note, doctor, of the paper and the date.'

'It is *The Morning Chronicle* of April 27, 1890. Just two months ago.'

'Very good. Now, Mr Wilson.'

'Well, it is just as I have been telling you, Mr Sherlock Holmes,' said Jabez Wilson, mopping his forehead, 'I have a small pawnbroker's business at Saxe-Coburg Square, near the City. It's not a very large affair, and of late years it has not done more than just give me a living. I used to be able to keep two assistants, but now I only keep one; and I would have a job to pay him but that he is willing to come for half wages, so as to learn the business.'

'What is the name of this obliging youth?' asked Sherlock Holmes.

'His name is Vincent Spaulding, and he's not such a youth either. It's hard to say his age. I should not wish a smarter assistant, Mr Holmes; and I know very well that he could better himself, and earn twice what I am able to give him. But, after all, if he is satisfied, why should I put ideas in his head?'

'Why, indeed? You seem most fortunate in having an employee who comes under the full market price. It is not a common experience among employers in this age. I don't know that your assistant is not as remarkable as your advertisement.'

'Oh, he has his faults, too,' said Mr Wilson. 'Never was such a fellow for photography. Snapping away with a camera when he ought to be improving his mind, and then diving down into the cellar like a rabbit into its hole to develop his pictures. That is his main fault; but, on the whole, he's a good worker. There's no vice in him.'

'He is still with you, I presume?'

'Yes, sir. He and a girl of fourteen, who does a bit of simple cooking, and keeps the place clean—that's all I have in the house, for I am a widower, and never had any family. We live very quietly, sir, the three of us; and we keep a roof over our heads, and pay our debts, if we do nothing more.'

'The first thing that put us out was that advertisement. Spaulding, he came down into the office just this day eight weeks before, with this very paper in his hand, and he says:

'I wish to the Lord, Mr Wilson, that I was a red-headed man.'

'Why that?' I asks.

'Why,' says he, 'here's another vacancy on the League of the Red-headed Men. It's worth quite a little fortune to any man who gets it, and I understand that there are more vacancies than there are men, so that the trustees are at their wits' end what to do with the money. If my hair would only change colour here's a nice little crib all ready for me to step into.'

'Why, what is it, then?' I asked. 'You see, Mr Holmes, I am a very stay-at-home man, and, as my business came to me instead of my having to go to it, I was often weeks on end without putting my foot over the door mat. In that way

I didn't know much of what was going on outside, and I was always glad of a bit of news.'

'Have you never heard of the League of the Red-headed Men?' he asked, with his eyes open.

'Never.'

'Why, I wonder at that, for you are eligible yourself for one of the vacancies.'

'And what are they worth?' I asked.

'Oh, merely a couple of hundred a year, but the work is slight, and it need not interfere very much with one's other occupations.'

'Well, you can easily think that that made me prick up my ears, for the business has not been over good for some years, and an extra couple of hundred would have been very handy.'

'Tell me all about it,' said I.

'Well,' said he, showing me the advertisement, 'you can see for yourself that the League has a vacancy, and there is the address where you should apply for particulars. As far as I can make out, the League was founded by an American millionaire, Ezekiah Hopkins, who was very peculiar in his ways. He was himself red-headed, and he had a great sympathy for all red-headed men; so, when he died, it was found that he had left his enormous fortune in the hands of trustees, with instructions to apply the interest to the providing of easy berths to men whose hair is of that colour. From all I hear it is splendid pay, and very little to do.'

'But,' said I, 'there would be millions of red-headed men who would apply.'

'Not so many as you might think,' he answered. 'You see

it is really confined to Londoners, and to grown men. This American had started from London when he was young, and he wanted to do the old town a good turn. Then, again, I have heard it is of no use your applying if your hair is light red, or dark red, or anything but real, bright, blazing, fiery red. Now, if you cared to apply, Mr Wilson, you would just walk in; but perhaps it would hardly be worth your while to put yourself out of the way for the sake of a few hundred pounds.'

'Now it is a fact, gentlemen, as you may see for yourselves, that my hair is of a very full and rich tint, so that it seemed to me that, if there was to be any competition in the matter, I stood as good a chance as any man that I had ever met. Vincent Spaulding seemed to know so much about it that I thought he might prove useful, so I just ordered him to put up the shutters for the day, and to come right away with me. He was very willing to have a holiday, so we shut the business up, and started off for the address that was given us in the advertisement.

'I never hope to see such a sight as that again, Mr Holmes. From north, south, east, and west every man who had a shade of red in his hair had tramped into the city to answer the advertisement. Fleet Street was choked with red-headed folk, and Pope's Court looked like a coster's orange barrow. I should not have thought there were so many in the whole country as were brought together by that single advertisement. Every shade of colour they were—straw, lemon, orange, brick, Irish setter, liver, clay; but, as Spaulding said, there were not many who had the real vivid flame-coloured tint. When I saw how many were waiting, I would have given it up in despair; but

Spaulding would not hear of it. How he did it I could not imagine, but he pushed and pulled and butted until he got me through the crowd, and right up to the steps which led to the office. There was a double stream upon the stair, some going up in hope, and some coming back dejected; but we wedged in as well as we could, and soon found ourselves in the office.'

'Your experience has been a most entertaining one,' remarked Holmes, as his client paused and refreshed his memory with a huge pinch of snuff. 'Pray continue your very interesting statement.'

'There was nothing in the office but a couple of wooden chairs and a deal table, behind which sat a small man, with a head that was even redder than mine. He said a few words to each candidate as he came up, and then he always managed to find some fault in them which would disqualify them. Getting a vacancy did not seem to be such a very easy matter after all. However, when our turn came, the little man was much more favourable to me than to any of the others, and he closed the door as we entered, so that he might have a private word with us.'

"This is Mr Jabez Wilson," said my assistant, "and he is willing to fill a vacancy in the League."

"And he is admirably suited for it," the other answered. "He has every requirement. I cannot recall when I have seen anything so fine." He took a step backward, cocked his head on one side, and gazed at my hair until I felt quite bashful. Then suddenly he plunged forward, wrung my hand, and congratulated me warmly on my success.

"It would be injustice to hesitate," said he. "You will, however, I am sure, excuse me for taking an obvious precaution." With that he seized my hair in both his hands, and tugged until I yelled with the pain. "There is water in your eyes," said he, as he released me. "I perceive that all is as it should be. But we have to be careful, for we have twice been deceived by wigs and once by paint. I could tell you tales of cobbler's wax which would disgust you with human nature." He stepped over to the window and shouted through it at the top of his voice that the vacancy was filled. A groan of disappointment came up from below, and the folk all trooped away in different directions, until there was not a red-head to be seen except my own and that of the manager.

"My name," said he, "is Mr Duncan Ross, and I am myself one of the pensioners upon the fund left by our noble benefactor. Are you a married man, Mr Wilson? Have you a family?"

I answered that I had not.

His face fell immediately.

"Dear me!" he said, gravely, "that is very serious indeed! I am sorry to hear you say that. The fund was, of course, for the propagation and spread of the red-heads as well as for their maintenance. It is exceedingly unfortunate that you should be a bachelor."

'My face lengthened at this, Mr Holmes, for I thought that I was not to have the vacancy after all; but, after thinking it over for a few minutes, he said that it would be all right.'

"In the case of another," said he, "the objection might be fatal, but we must stretch a point in favour of a man with such a head of hair as yours. When shall you be able to enter upon your new duties?"

'Well, it is a little awkward, for I have a business already,' said I.

'"Oh, never mind about that, Mr Wilson!" said Vincent Spaulding. "I shall be able to look after that for you."

"What would be the hours?" I asked.

"Ten to two."

'Now a pawnbroker's business is mostly done of an evening, Mr Holmes, especially Thursday and Friday evenings, which is just before pay day; so it would suit me very well to earn a little in the mornings. Besides, I knew that my assistant was a good man, and that he would see to anything that turned up.'

"That would suit me very well," said I. "And the pay?"

"Is four pounds a week."

"And the work?"

"Is purely nominal."

"What do you call purely nominal?"

"Well, you have to be in the office, or at least in the building, the whole time. If you leave, you forfeit your whole position forever. The will is very clear upon that point. You don't comply with the conditions if you budge from the office during that time."

'It's only four hours a day, and I should not think of leaving,' said I.

"No excuse will avail," said Mr Duncan Ross, "neither sickness, nor business, nor anything else. There you must stay, or you lose your billet."

"And the work?"

"Is to copy out the 'Encyclopaedia Britannica.'" There is the first volume of it in that press. You must find your own ink, pens, and blotting paper, but we provide this table and chair. Will you be ready tomorrow?"

"Certainly," I answered.

"Then, goodbye, Mr Jabez Wilson, and let me congratulate you once more on the important position which you have been fortunate enough to gain." He bowed me out of the room, and I went home with my assistant hardly knowing what to say or do, I was so pleased at my own good fortune.

'Well, I thought over the matter all day, and by evening I was in low spirits again; for I had quite persuaded myself that the whole affair must be some great hoax or fraud, though what its object might be I could not imagine. It seemed altogether past belief that anyone could make such a will, or that they would pay such a sum for doing anything so simple as copying out the 'Encyclopaedia Britannica.' Vincent Spaulding did what he could to cheer me up, but by bedtime I had reasoned myself out of the whole thing. However, in the morning I determined to have a look at it anyhow, so I bought a penny bottle of ink, and with a quill pen and seven sheets of foolscap paper I started off for Pope's Court.

'Well, to my surprise and delight everything was as right as possible. The table was set out ready for me, and Mr Duncan Ross was there to see that I got fairly to work. He started me off upon the letter A, and then he left me; but he would drop in from time to time to see that all was right with me. At two o'clock he bade me good day, complimented me upon the amount that I had written, and locked the door of the office after me.

'This went on day after day, Mr Holmes, and on Saturday the manager came in and planked down four golden sovereigns for my week's work. It was the same next week, and the same the week after. Every morning I was there at ten, and every afternoon I left at two. By degrees Mr Duncan Ross took to coming in only once of a morning, and then, after a time, he did not come in at all. Still, of course, I never dared to leave the room for an instant, for I was not sure when he might come, and the billet was such a good one, and suited me so well, that I would not risk the loss of it.

'Eight weeks passed away like this, and I had written about Abbots, and Archery, and Armour, and Architecture, and Attica, and hoped with diligence that I might get on to the Bs before very long. It cost me something in foolscap, and I had pretty nearly filled a shelf with my writings. And then suddenly the whole business came to an end.'

'To an end?'

'Yes, sir. And no later than this morning. I went to my work as usual at ten o'clock, but the door was shut and locked, with a little square of cardboard hammered onto the middle of the panel with a tack. Here it is, and you can read for yourself.'

He held up a piece of white cardboard, about the size of a sheet of note paper. It read in this fashion:

'THE RED-HEADED LEAGUE IS DISSOLVED.
Oct. 9, 1890.'

Sherlock Holmes and I surveyed this curt announcement and the rueful face behind it, until the comical side of the affair so completely overtopped every consideration that we both burst out into a roar of laughter.

'I cannot see that there is anything very funny,' cried our client, flushing up to the roots of his flaming head. 'If you can do nothing better than laugh at me, I can go elsewhere.'

'No, no,' cried Holmes, shoving him back into the chair from which he had half risen. 'I really wouldn't miss your case for the world. It is most refreshingly unusual. But there is, if you will excuse my saying so, something just a little funny about it. Pray what steps did you take when you found the card upon the door?'

'I was staggered, sir. I did not know what to do. Then I called at the offices round, but none of them seemed to know anything about it. Finally, I went to the landlord, who is an accountant living on the ground floor, and I asked him if he could tell me what had become of the Red-headed League. He said that he had never heard of any such body. Then I asked him who Mr Duncan Ross was. He answered that the name was new to him.

'Well,' said I, 'the gentleman at No. 4.'

"What, the red-headed man?"

"Yes."

"Oh," said he, "his name was William Morris. He was a solicitor, and was using my room as a temporary convenience until his new premises were ready. He moved out yesterday."

"Where could I find him?"

"Oh, at his new offices. He did tell me the address. Yes, 17 King Edward Street, near St. Paul's."

'I started off, Mr Holmes, but when I got to that address it was a manufactory of artificial knee-caps, and no one in it had ever heard of either Mr William Morris or Mr Duncan Ross.'

'And what did you do then?' asked Holmes.

'I went home to Saxe-Coburg Square, and I took the advice of my assistant. But he could not help me in any way. He could only say that if I waited I should hear by post. But that was not quite good enough, Mr Holmes. I did not wish to lose such a place without a struggle, so, as I had heard that you were good enough to give advice to poor folk who were in need of it, I came right away to you.'

'And you did very wisely,' said Holmes. 'Your case is an exceedingly remarkable one, and I shall be happy to look into it. From what you have told me I think that it is possible that graver issues hang from it than might at first sight appear.'

'Grave enough!' said Mr Jabez Wilson. 'Why, I have lost four pound a week!'

'As far as you are personally concerned,' remarked Holmes, 'I do not see that you have any grievance against this extraordinary league. On the contrary, you are, as I understand, richer by some thirty pounds, to say nothing of the minute knowledge which you have gained on every subject which comes under the letter A. You have lost nothing by them.'

'No, sir. But I want to find out about them, and who they are, and what their object was in playing this prank—if it was a prank—upon me. It was a pretty expensive joke for them, for it cost them two-and-thirty pounds.'

'We shall endeavour to clear up these points for you. And, first, one or two questions, Mr Wilson. This assistant of yours who first called your attention to the advertisement—how long had he been with you?'

'About a month then.'

'How did he come?'

'In answer to an advertisement.'

'Was he the only applicant?'

'No, I had a dozen.'

'Why did you pick him?'

'Because he was handy and would come cheap.'

'At half wages, in fact.'

'Yes.'

'What is he like, this Vincent Spaulding?'

'Small, stout-built, very quick in his ways, no hair on his face, though he's not short of thirty. Has a white splash of acid upon his forehead.'

Holmes sat up in his chair in considerable excitement. 'I thought as much,' said he. 'Have you ever observed that his ears are pierced for earrings?'

'Yes, sir. He told me that a gypsy had done it for him when he was a lad.'

'Hum!' said Holmes, sinking back in deep thought. 'He is still with you?'

'Oh, yes, sir; I have only just left him.'

'And has your business been attended to in your absence?'

'Nothing to complain of, sir. There's never very much to do of a morning.'

'That will do, Mr Wilson. I shall be happy to give you an opinion upon the subject in the course of a day or two. Today is Saturday, and I hope that by Monday we may come to a conclusion.'

'Well, Watson,' said Holmes, when our visitor had left us, 'what do you make of it all?'

'I make nothing of it,' I answered frankly. 'It is a most mysterious business.'

'As a rule,' said Holmes, 'the more bizarre a thing is the less mysterious it proves to be. It is your commonplace, featureless crimes which are really puzzling, just as a commonplace face is the most difficult to identify. But I must be prompt over this matter.'

'What are you going to do, then?' I asked.

'To smoke,' he answered. 'It is quite a three-pipe problem, and I beg that you won't speak to me for fifty minutes.' He curled himself up in his chair, with his thin knees drawn up to his hawklike nose, and there he sat with his eyes closed and his black clay pipe thrusting out like the bill of some strange bird. I had come to the conclusion that he had dropped asleep, and indeed was nodding myself, when he suddenly sprang out of his chair with the gesture of a man who has made up his mind, and put his pipe down upon the mantelpiece.

'Sarasate plays at St. James's Hall this afternoon,' he remarked. 'What do you think, Watson? Could your patients spare you for a few hours?'

'I have nothing to do today. My practice is never very absorbing.'

'Then put on your hat and come. I am going through the city first, and we can have some lunch on the way. I observe that there is a good deal of German music on the programme, which is rather more to my taste than Italian or French. It is introspective, and I want to introspect. Come along!'

We travelled by the Underground as far as Aldersgate; and a short walk took us to Saxe-Coburg Square, the scene of the singular story which we had listened to in the morning. It was a poky, little, shabby-genteel place, where four lines of dingy, two-storied brick houses looked out into a small railed-in enclosure, where a lawn of weedy grass, and a few clumps of faded laurel bushes made a hard fight against a smoke-laden and uncongenial atmosphere. Three gilt balls and a brown board with JABEZ WILSON in white letters, upon a corner house, announced the place where our red-headed client carried on his business.

Sherlock Holmes stopped in front of it with his head on one side, and looked it all over, with his eyes shining brightly between puckered lids. Then he walked slowly up the street, and then down again to the corner, still looking keenly at the houses. Finally he returned to the pawnbroker's and, having thumped vigorously upon the pavement with his stick two or three times, he went up to the door and knocked. It was instantly opened by a bright-looking, clean-shaven young fellow, who asked him to step in.

'Thank you,' said Holmes, 'I only wished to ask you how you would go from here to the Strand.'

'Third right, fourth left,' answered the assistant, promptly, closing the door.

'Smart fellow, that,' observed Holmes as we walked away. 'He is, in my judgment, the fourth smartest man in London, and for daring I am not sure that he has not a claim to be third. I have known something of him before.'

'Evidently,' said I, 'Mr Wilson's assistant counts for a good deal in this mystery of the Red-headed League. I am sure that you inquired your way merely in order that you might see him.'

'Not him.'

'What then?'

'The knees of his trousers.'

'And what did you see?'

'What I expected to see.'

'Why did you beat the pavement?'

'My dear doctor, this is a time for observation, not for talk. We are spies in an enemy's country. We know something of Saxe-Coburg Square. Let us now explore the parts which lie behind it.'

The road in which we found ourselves as we turned round the corner from the retired Saxe-Coburg Square presented as great a contrast to it as the front of a picture does to the back. It was one of the main arteries which convey the traffic of the city to the north and west. The roadway was blocked with the immense stream of commerce flowing in a double tide inward and outward, while the footpaths were black with the hurrying swarm of pedestrians. It was difficult to realize, as we looked at the line of fine shops and stately business premises, that they really abutted on the other side upon the faded and stagnant square which we had just quitted.

'Let me see,' said Holmes, standing at the corner, and glancing along the line, 'I should like just to remember the order of the houses here. It is a hobby of mine to have an exact knowledge of London. There is Mortimer's, the tobacconist; the little newspaper shop, the Coburg branch of the City and

Suburban Bank, the Vegetarian Restaurant, and McFarlane's carriage-building depot. That carries us right on to the other block. And now, doctor, we've done our work, so it's time we had some play. A sandwich and a cup of coffee, and then off to violin-land, where all is sweetness, and delicacy, and harmony, and there are no red-headed clients to vex us with their conundrums.'

My friend was an enthusiastic musician, being himself not only a very capable performer, but a composer of no ordinary merit. All the afternoon he sat in the stalls wrapped in the most perfect happiness, gently waving his long thin fingers in time to the music, while his gently smiling face and his languid, dreamy eyes were as unlike those of Holmes the sleuth-hound, Holmes the relentless, keen-witted, ready-handed criminal agent, as it was possible to conceive.

In his singular character the dual nature alternately asserted itself, and his extreme exactness and astuteness represented, as I have often thought, the reaction against the poetic and contemplative mood which occasionally predominated in him. The swing of his nature took him from extreme languor to devouring energy; and, as I knew well, he was never so truly formidable as when, for days on end, he had been lounging in his armchair amid his improvisations and his black-letter editions. Then it was that the lust of the chase would suddenly come upon him, and that his brilliant reasoning power would rise to the level of intuition, until those who were unacquainted with his methods would look askance at him as on a man whose knowledge was not that of other mortals. When I saw him that afternoon so enwrapped in the music at St. James's Hall, I felt that an evil time might be coming upon those whom he had set himself to hunt down.

'You want to go home, no doubt, doctor,' he remarked, as we emerged.

'Yes, it would be as well.'

'And I have some business to do which will take some hours. This business at Saxe-Coburg Square is serious.'

'Why serious?'

'A considerable crime is in contemplation. I have every reason to believe that we shall be in time to stop it. But today being Saturday rather complicates matters. I shall want your help tonight.'

'At what time?'

'Ten will be early enough.'

'I shall be at Baker Street at ten.'

'Very well. And, I say, doctor! There may be some little-danger, so kindly put your army revolver in your pocket.' He waved his hand, turned on his heel, and disappeared in an instant among the crowd.

I trust that I am not more dense than my neighbours, but I was always oppressed with a sense of my own stupidity in my dealings with Sherlock Holmes. Here I had heard what he had heard, I had seen what he had seen, and yet from his words it was evident that he saw clearly not only what had happened, but what was about to happen, while to me the whole business was still confusing and grotesque. As I drove home to my house in Kensington I thought over it all, from the extraordinary story of the red-headed copier of the 'Encyclopaedia' down to the visit to Saxe-Coburg Square, and the ominous words with which he had parted from me. What was this nocturnal expedition, and why should I go armed? Where were we going, and what were we to do? I had the hint from Holmes that this smooth-faced pawnbroker's assistant was a formidable man—a man who might play a deep game. I tried to puzzle it out, but gave it up in despair, and set the matter aside until night should bring an explanation.

It was quarter-past nine when I started from home and made my way across the Park, and so through Oxford Street to Baker Street. Two hansoms were standing at the door, and, as I entered the passage, I heard the sound of voices from above. On entering his room, I found Holmes in animated conversation with two men, one of whom I recognized as Peter Jones, the official police agent; while the other was a long, thin, sad-faced man, with a very shiny hat and oppressively respectable frock coat.

'Ha! Our party is complete,' said Holmes, buttoning up his peajacket, and taking his heavy hunting crop from the rack. 'Watson, I think you know Mr Jones, of Scotland Yard? Let me introduce you to Mr Merryweather, who is to be our companion in tonight's adventure.'

'We're hunting in couples again, doctor, you see,' said Jones, in his consequential way. 'Our friend here is a wonderful man for starting a chase. All he wants is an old dog to help him do the running down.'

'I hope a wild goose may not prove to be the end of our chase,' observed Mr Merryweather gloomily.

'You may place considerable confidence in Mr Holmes, sir,' said the police agent loftily. 'He has his own little methods, which are, if he won't mind my saying so, just a little too theoretical and fantastic, but he has the makings of a detective in him. It is not too much to say that once or twice, as in that business of the Sholto murder and the Agra treasure, he has been more nearly correct than the official force.'

'Oh, if you say so, Mr Jones, it is all right!' said the stranger, with deference. 'Still, I confess that I miss my rubber. It is the first Saturday night for seven-and-twenty years that I have not had my rubber.'

'I think you will find,' said Sherlock Holmes, 'that you will play for a higher stake tonight than you have ever done yet, and that the play will be more exciting. For you, Mr Merryweather, the stake will be some thirty thousand pounds; and for you, Jones, it will be the man upon whom you wish to lay your hands.'

'John Clay, the murderer, thief, smasher, and forger. He's a young man, Mr Merryweather, but he is at the head of his profession, and I would rather have my bracelets on him than on any criminal in London. He's a remarkable man, is young John Clay. His grandfather was a Royal Duke, and he himself has been to Eton and Oxford. His brain is as cunning as his fingers, and though we meet signs of him at every turn, we never know where to find the man himself. He'll crack a crib in Scotland one week, and be raising money to build an orphanage in Cornwall the next. I've been on his track for years, and have never set eyes on him yet.'

'I hope that I may have the pleasure of introducing you tonight. I've had one or two little turns also with Mr John Clay, and I agree with you that he is at the head of his profession.

It is past ten, however, and quite time that we started. If you two will take the first hansom, Watson and I will follow in the second.'

Sherlock Holmes was not very communicative during the long drive, and lay back in the cab humming the tunes which he had heard in the afternoon. We rattled through an endless labyrinth of gaslit streets until we emerged into Farringdon Street.

'We are close there now,' my friend remarked. 'This fellow Merryweather is a bank director and personally interested in the matter. I thought it as well to have Jones with us also. He is not a bad fellow, though an absolute imbecile in his profession. He has one positive virtue. He is as brave as a bulldog, and as tenacious as a lobster if he gets his claws upon anyone. Here we are, and they are waiting for us.'

We had reached the same crowded thoroughfare in which we had found ourselves in the morning. Our cabs were dismissed, and following the guidance of Mr Merryweather, we passed down a narrow passage, and through a side door which he opened for us. Within there was a small corridor, which ended in a very massive iron gate. This also was opened, and led down a flight of winding stone steps, which terminated at another formidable gate. Mr Merryweather stopped to light a lantern, and then conducted us down a dark, earth-smelling passage, and so, after opening a third door, into a huge vault or cellar, which was piled all round with crates and massive boxes.

'You are not very vulnerable from above,' Holmes remarked, as he held up the lantern and gazed about him.

'Nor from below,' said Mr Merryweather, striking his stick upon the flags which lined the floor. 'Why, dear me, it sounds quite hollow!' he remarked, looking up in surprise.

'I must really ask you to be a little more quiet,' said Holmes severely. 'You have already imperiled the whole success of our expedition. Might I beg that you would have the goodness to sit down upon one of those boxes, and not to interfere?'

The solemn Mr Merryweather perched himself upon a crate, with a very injured expression upon his face, while Holmes fell upon his knees upon the floor, and, with the lantern and a magnifying lens, began to examine minutely the cracks between the stones. A few seconds sufficed to satisfy him, for he sprang to his feet again, and put his glass in his pocket.

'We have at least an hour before us,' he remarked, 'for they can hardly take any steps until the good pawnbroker is safely in bed. Then they will not lose a minute, for the sooner they do their work the longer time they will have for their escape. We are at present, doctor—as no doubt you have divined—in the cellar of the city branch of one of the principal London banks. Mr Merryweather is the chairman of directors, and he will explain to you that there are reasons why the more daring criminals of London should take a considerable interest in this cellar at present.'

'It is our French gold,' whispered the director. 'We have had several warnings that an attempt might be made upon it.'

'Your French gold?'

'Yes. We had occasion some months ago to strengthen our resources, and borrowed, for that purpose, thirty thousand napoleons from the Bank of France. It has become known that we have never had occasion to unpack the money, and that it is still lying in our cellar. The crate upon which I sit contains two thousand napoleons packed between layers of lead foil. Our reserve of bullion is much larger at present than is usually kept in a single branch office, and the directors have had misgivings upon the subject.'

'Which were very well-justified,' observed Holmes. 'And now it is time that we arranged our little plans. I expect that within an hour matters will come to a head. In the meantime, Mr Merryweather, we must put the screen over that dark lantern.'

'And sit in the dark?'

'I am afraid so. I had brought a pack of cards in my pocket, and I thought that, as we were a partie carree, you might have your rubber after all. But I see that the enemy's preparations have gone so far that we cannot risk the presence of a light. And, first of all, we must choose our positions. These are daring men, and, though we shall take them at a disadvantage, they may do us some harm, unless we are careful. I shall stand behind this crate, and you conceal yourself behind those. Then, when I flash a light upon them, close in swiftly. If they fire, Watson, have no compunction about shooting them down.'

I placed my revolver, cocked, upon the top of the wooden case behind which I crouched. Holmes shot the slide across the front of his lantern, and left us in pitch darkness—such an absolute darkness as I have never before experienced. The smell of hot metal remained to assure us that the light was still there, ready to flash out at a moment's notice. To me, with my nerves worked up to a pitch of expectancy, there was something depressing and subduing in the sudden gloom, and in the cold, dank air of the vault.

'They have but one retreat,' whispered Holmes. 'That is back through the house into Saxe-Coburg Square. I hope that you have done what I asked you, Jones?'

'I have an inspector and two officers waiting at the front door.'

'Then we have stopped all the holes. And now we must be silent and wait.'

What a time it seemed! From comparing notes afterwards, it was but an hour and a quarter, yet it appeared to me that the night must have almost gone, and the dawn be breaking above us. My limbs were weary and stiff, for I feared to change my position, yet my nerves were worked up to the highest pitch of tension, and my hearing was so acute that I could not only hear the gentle breathing of my companions, but I could distinguish the deeper, heavier inbreath of the bulky Jones from the thin, sighing note of the bank director. From my position I could look over the case in the direction of the floor. Suddenly my eyes caught the glint of a light.

At first it was but a lurid spark upon the stone pavement. Then it lengthened out until it became a yellow line, and then, without any warning or sound, a gash seemed to open and a hand appeared, a white, almost womanly hand, which felt about in the centre of the little area of light. For a minute or more the hand, with its writhing fingers, protruded out of the floor. Then it was withdrawn as suddenly as it appeared, and all was dark again save the single lurid spark, which marked a chink between the stones.

Its disappearance, however, was but momentary. With a rending, tearing sound, one of the broad white stones turned over upon its side, and left a square, gaping hole, through which streamed the light of a lantern. Over the edge there peeped a clean-cut, boyish face, which looked keenly about it, and then, with a hand on either side of the aperture, drew itself shoulder-high and waist-high, until one knee rested upon the edge. In another instant he stood at the side of the hole, and was hauling after him a companion, lithe and small like himself, with a pale face and a shock of very red hair.

'It's all clear,' he whispered. 'Have you the chisel and the bags? Great Scott! Jump, Archie, jump, and I'll swing for it!'

Sherlock Holmes had sprung out and seized the intruder by the collar. The other dived down the hole, and I heard the sound of rending cloth as Jones clutched at his skirts. The light flashed upon the barrel of a revolver, but Holmes's hunting crop came down on the man's wrist, and the pistol clinked upon the stone floor.

'It's no use, John Clay,' said Holmes blandly, 'you have no chance at all.'

'So I see,' the other answered, with the utmost coolness. 'I fancy that my pal is all right, though I see you have got his coat-tails.'

'There are three men waiting for him at the door,' said Holmes.

'Oh, indeed. You seem to have done the thing very completely. I must compliment you.'

'And I you,' Holmes answered. 'Your red-headed idea was very new and effective.'

'You'll see your pal again presently,' said Jones. 'He's quicker at climbing down holes than I am. Just hold out while I fix the derbies.'

'I beg that you will not touch me with your filthy hands,' remarked our prisoner, as the handcuffs clattered upon his wrists. 'You may not be aware that I have royal blood in my veins. Have the goodness also, when you address me, always to say 'sir' and 'please.''

'All right,' said Jones, with a stare and a snigger. 'Well, would you please, sir, march upstairs where we can get a cab to carry your highness to the police station?'

'That is better,' said John Clay serenely. He made a sweeping bow to the three of us, and walked quietly off in the custody of the detective.

'Really, Mr Holmes,' said Mr Merryweather, as we followed them from the cellar, 'I do not know how the bank can thank you or repay you. There is no doubt that you have detected and defeated in the most complete manner one of the most determined attempts at bank robbery that have ever come within my experience.'

'I have had one or two little scores of my own to settle with Mr John Clay,' said Holmes. 'I have been at some small expense over this matter, which I shall expect the bank to refund, but beyond that I am amply repaid by having had an experience which is in many ways unique, and by hearing the very remarkable narrative of the Red-headed League.'

'You see, Watson,' he explained, in the early hours of

the morning, as we sat over a glass of whisky and soda in Baker Street, 'it was perfectly obvious from the first that the only possible object of this rather fantastic business of the advertisement of the League, and the copying of the 'Encyclopaedia,' must be to get this not so over-bright pawnbroker out of the way for a number of hours every day. It was a curious way of managing it, but really it would be difficult to suggest a better. The method was no doubt suggested to Clay's ingenious mind by the colour of his accomplice's hair. The four pounds a week was a lure which must draw him, and what was it to them, who were playing for thousands? They put in the advertisement, one rogue has the temporary office, the other rogue incites the man to apply for it, and together they manage to secure his absence every morning in the week. From the time that I heard of the assistant having come for half wages, it was obvious to me that he had some strong motive for securing the situation.'

'But how could you guess what the motive was?'

'Had there been women in the house, I should have suspected a mere vulgar intrigue. That, however, was out of the question. The man's business was a small one, and there was nothing in his house which could account for such elabourate preparations, and such an expenditure as they were at. It must then be something out of the house. What could it be? I thought of the assistant's fondness for photography, and his trick of vanishing into the cellar. The cellar! There was the end of this tangled clew. Then I made inquiries as to this mysterious assistant, and found that I had to deal with one of the coolest and most daring criminals in London. He was doing something in the cellar—something which took many hours a day for months on end. What could it be, once more? I could think of nothing save that he was running a tunnel to some other building.'

'So far I had got when we went to visit the scene of action. I surprised you by beating upon the pavement with my stick. I was ascertaining whether the cellar stretched out in front or behind. It was not in front. Then I rang the bell, and, as I hoped, the assistant answered it. We have had some skirmishes, but we had never set eyes upon each other before. I hardly looked at his face. His knees were what I wished to see. You must yourself have remarked how worn, wrinkled, and stained they were. They spoke of those hours of burrowing. The only remaining point was what they were burrowing for. I walked round the corner, saw that the City and Suburban Bank abutted on our friend's premises, and felt that I had solved my problem. When you drove home after the concert I called upon Scotland Yard, and upon the chairman of the bank directors, with the result that you have seen.'

'And how could you tell that they would make their attempt tonight?' I asked.

'Well, when they closed their League offices that was a sign that they cared no longer about Mr Jabez Wilson's presence; in other words, that they had completed their tunnel. But it was essential that they should use it soon, as it might be discovered, or the bullion might be removed. Saturday would suit them better than any other day, as it would give them two days for their escape. For all these reasons I expected them to come tonight.'

'You reasoned it out beautifully,' I exclaimed, in unfeigned admiration. 'It is so long a chain, and yet every link rings true.'

'It saved me from ennui,' he answered, yawning. 'Alas! I already feel it closing in upon me. My life is spent in one long effort to escape from the commonplaces of existence. These little problems help me to do so.'

'And you are a benefactor of the race,' said I. He shrugged his shoulders. 'Well, perhaps, after all, it is of some little use,' he remarked. 'L'homme c'est rien—l'oeuvre c'est tout,' as Gustave Flaubert wrote to Georges Sands.'

The Dare

Beverley Naidoo

MARIKA THRUST the glass jar up to Veronica's face.

'See this one Nicky!' she declared. 'Caught it last week!'
Veronica stared at the coiled brown shape slithering inside
the greenish liquid. She felt sick.

'You should have seen how blinking quick I was, man!
This sort are poisonous!'

Marika's eyes pinned her down, watching for a reaction.
She didn't know which were worse. Marika's or those of the
dead creature in the jar.

'Where did you find it?'

Her voice did not betray her and Marika began her
dramatic tale about tracking the snake in the bougainvillea
next to the hen-run.

It was a valuable addition to her collection. Rows of
bottles, all with the same green liquid, lined the shelf above
her bed. Spiders and insects of various shapes and sizes

floated safely, serenely, inside. Marika carefully replaced the snake next to another prize item—a one-legged chameleon, its colours dulled and fixed. Veronica remembered it alive. It had been the farm children's pet briefly until they had got tired of capturing flies for it. She had even helped one whole Saturday, prowling around the cowshed, sneaking up and snapping the overfed blue-buzzers in cigarette tins. The next morning Marika and her brothers had decided to let the creature go free and get its own dinner. But when they had come to release the catch of the splintering old wood-and-wire hutch, the chameleon lay stiff and still. The three boys had wanted to make a special grave down in the donga—but in the end Marika had persuaded them to let her preserve it.

The farm, a small-holding owned by Marika's parents, lay against a mountain in the middle of the Magaliesburg. As well as growing fruit and vegetables and keeping a few animals, the van Reenens let out a small cottage on the farm, mostly to city visitors. It was near enough to Johannesburg for Mr and Mrs Martin with their only child Veronica to get away from the ever-increasing hustle for short breaks. They were regulars, coming two or three times a year. In fact Mr Martin had been visiting since he was a child, when Marika's mother herself had been a small girl on the same farm. Veronica's own memories of the place stretched back for as long as she could remember. For years she and Marika had played 'house' in the donga behind the farmhouse. They had used larger stones for the walls, shifting around smaller stones as the furniture. In the past Veronica used to bring all her dolls, despite her mother's protests. Sensing Marika's envy, she had enjoyed saying which dolls could be played with. But since Marika's tenth birthday things were different.

Veronica had been taken by surprise. She had been sitting with the farm children on the wall of the stoep, dangling her legs and kicking the brickwork with her heels like the others. Marika had been telling her about her birthday treat when Veronica had suggested that they go to the donga.

'Hey, the girls are going to play dollies!' Marika's twin brother Piet had sneered. Slipping off the wall, six year old Dirk had rolled on the ground, kicking his legs in the air and cooing.

'Gaga gaga! Mommy! Mommy! Change my nappy!'

Veronica had glared at him and he had pulled a face at her. She had fought to hold back her tears. Only Anton, the oldest, had not joined in, but called the others to leave the girls alone to their sissy games. Marika had reacted furiously.

'I'm not a sissy!' she had screamed after them.

Leaving Veronica alone on the stoep, she had gone inside the house, slamming the door behind her.

When Veronica returned to the farm a few months later, Marika had begun her bottle collection. Veronica had also left her dolls at home, except for the eyelid clicking, brown-eyed Margaret. But this time the porcelain head with brown painted curls remained tucked under the bedclothes and was spoken to only at night. She became Veronica's personal counsellor on the farm—a pale replica of Veronica's personal counsellor in town.

Back home, in Johannesburg it was Rebecca, their maid, to whom Veronica confided. She was a far better listener than Margaret because she made sympathetic noises. With Veronica's mother often helping out at her father's office, or busy with Mothers' Union meetings, they spent a lot of time together. Whether she was cooking, washing, ironing or dusting, Rebecca was always prepared to chat. But she never came to the farm with them. Instead she went to visit her own children, living with their grandmother, a five-hour bus ride away.

Sharing secrets with Rebecca was fun, especially when Rebecca had let her visit her dim, tiny room in the servants' quarters at the top of their block of flats. It had started with her desperate desire to see the bedspread which Rebecca had been patiently embroidering for months on 'babysitting' nights when Veronica's parents went out. Although Veronica didn't think she needed to be 'babysat', she liked Rebecca's company. Together, they would sit and talk at the table in the Martin's kitchen until it was her bedtime. She had watched the bedspread growing and when it was finally completed, had begged and nagged to see how it looked on the bed. But before she could be taken, Rebecca had made her promise, 'Remember, you are not to tell your ma or pa!'

Because it had been a secret, everything had stayed fixed in her mind like a picture. The splendid bedcover was draped over an old iron bed raised up high on bricks. A curtain across one corner of the room, Rebecca's cupboard. An orange crate table next to the bed, on which stood a photo of Rebecca's four children. Veronica had studied their smiling black faces to see if they looked like their mother, trying to match the faces to the names she asked Rebecca to repeat. The only one whose name she always remembered was Selo, the oldest, because he was exactly her age and his name was shorter than the others.

'Is this Selo?' she had asked, picking out the tallest of the children, who had a cheerful, cheeky grin.

'Oh yes, that's Selo! Always getting into trouble!' Rebecca had laughed, adding, 'But he's a good boy.'

Yet here on the farm there was no Rebecca. So it was to Margaret that Veronica confided about the snake's awful eyes. Of course if it was Rebecca, she would make some sounds to show how disgusted she was. Then they would laugh together at how stupid it was to keep all those dead creatures in jars.

But there was something even more important she needed to talk to Rebecca about. It was something Marika had said after she had put the snake back on the shelf. She had hinted strongly that her brothers had made up a test which Veronica would have to pass before she could go on playing with them. Marika herself had carried out a dare set by the boys. She would not say what it had been, it was so terrible. She was equally mysterious about Veronica's dare.

'I'm not allowed to tell…but you know our neighbour Jan Venter?…'

Marika had stopped and ominously refused to say anything more.

Big and burly—known for his flaming red beard, moustache and temper—children, and even adults, usually kept clear of Meneer Venter when possible. Veronica had seen him only once, when he had called to see Mr van Reenen to insist Marika's father mend the fence between them. He ran one of the biggest orange estates in the area and everyone knew that he threatened to shoot any trespasser on his land like he shot baboons. That was not to be taken lightly. Jan Venter was known to be 'fond of the bottle' and there had been talk about the disappearance of Mrs Venter a few years ago. Some people said she just had enough of his temper and had gone back to her own people in another part of the country. The rumour amongst the local children was that he had murdered his wife and buried her in front of his house—under a poinsettia bush which now had more than usual brighter red flowers.

The next morning, instead of darting off early to look for Marika, Veronica hung back and waited for her parents before going to the farmhouse for breakfast. Marika and her family ate in the kitchen but the Martins were served their meals in the dining room, beneath a pair of massive kudu horns and heavily framed photographs of Marika's grandparents. Mrs van Reenen followed behind the servant who carried the plates of steaming porridge.

'Still no sign of rain, but it'll be a nice day again for you all!'

She smiled and stopped to pass on some of the local news, including talk of a leopard seen again on the mountain behind the farm.

Today Veronica took her time. When she came to her last piece of toast, she chewed it slowly. She was trying to think of a good reason to stay with her parents who were pouring second cups of coffee, when her mother said, 'You can be excused, Veronica dear. You can go off and play. You won't go near the mountain, will you?'

She nodded, pursing her lips together and got up. Her father ruffled her hair as she passed.

'Have a good day, Ronnie!'

He only called her that when he was relaxed. She just hoped Marika's brothers didn't ever hear it. Their jokes about 'Nicky' were bad enough.

Hoping the van Reenen children might still be at breakfast in the kitchen, Veronica headed for the opposite door, to the stoep. But they were already there on the wall, legs swinging, waiting. Anton, the oldest, was direct.

'We've made a new rule. Girls have to do a dare before they join our gang.'

Veronica stood rooted to the concrete floor. All the children except Anton were grinning. Dead-pan, he went on to explain that she had to climb through the barbed wire fence into the neighbouring Venter estate and make her way across to the front of Jan Venter's farmhouse.

'You've got to get one of his poinsettia flowers. We don't have any this side, so you can't cheat!'

They would accompany her as far as the fence and wait for her to return.

There was no way out. If she wasn't part of the gang, there would be no-one to play with. As they marched across the donga Veronica glanced at the spot where they used to play 'house' in the shade of the thorn trees. The stones were still there. It was like another world. Inside she felt cold and shivery even though her feet and arms were moving swiftly in step with the others and the sun's heat was already enveloping them. As they trudged in silence along the edge of the mealie field, nearing the wire fence, Dirk suddenly broke out into a jingle.

'Nicky, Nicky, looks so sicky!'

He was told sharply to shut up by the others.

'A dare is not a game! It's a serious thing you idiot,' Marika snapped.

At the fence, Anton and Piet parted the barbed wire for Veronica to slip through. Anton pointed.

'The farmhouse is that way. At the end of the orange trees follow the road.'

Veronica cast a quick glimpse back at the group. They all had solemn faces except for Dirk who couldn't hide his little grin. She was already far down the line of orange trees when she heard Marika's voice ringing faintly behind her.

'Good luck, hey Nicky!'

Sounds of laughter seemed to follow.

For as far as she could see ahead there were only straight rows of trees, the deep green leaves and bright orange fruit silently glinting in the sunlight. They were not good cover. With her shadow darting from one tree's patch of shade to the next, her mind began searching wildly for what to say if she was caught. Could she pretend she was lost…or that she had a dog which had got lost? Or that she had come to warn Meneer Venter about the leopard on the mountain? Veronica could not imagine the big burly man with the flaming beard believing any of her stories. She almost wished the dare had been for her to go up the mountain instead.

Her mouth was dry, her body wet and sticky, her legs sprinting heavily. Sucking in small quick breaths, she jerked to a halt. The moments of rest brought a terrible panic. What on earth was she doing here, alone in the middle of Jan Venter's oranges? This dare was too dangerous. She should run back and tell the others it was unfair. She bet they wouldn't do it! Then she remembered Marika saying her own dare was too terrible to talk about. Perhaps she had just said that to frighten her… but if she went back now, that would be the end of their friendship. Whatever could she do by herself on the farm? It wasn't worth thinking about. Lips pressed together, her eyes intently scoured the bushes ahead.

At last she could see she was coming to a dirt road. Peering from behind a tree, she studied how to make her way up it. On either side was a line of tall grey bluegums leading to a cluster of white-washed buildings. The furthest one seemed to be the main house. There was no poinsettia in sight, so the front had to be around one of the other sides. Behind the bluegums on the far side of the road, set a little back, were some huts—servants' quarters. Usually she hardly took any notice of these kind of buildings. They were just there, part of what you found on a farm. But now she was forced to scan the area around the huts very closely. Although there were some open doorways, they were too dark to see inside. No-one seemed to be around, either on the road or in the workers' compound, but it would be safer to stay on the side where she was for as long as possible. A few large avocado trees would provide thick cover for a short stretch—and then she would have to trust to the bluegums and to fortune.

At last, in line with the main house, she crossed the road. Her shoes smacking against the sand pounded as loudly as her heart. Facing her was a door, leading to a backyard. She ducked down to creep past a window. A few paces more and she had reached the side of the raised stoep. On tip-toe she stretched to look. Still no-one! Through the wooden railings she glimpsed a spray of pointed red flowers. The poinsettia was just around the corner! Making a final dash to the bush, she ripped off a flower at the stem. Milky white stuff spurted out onto her fingers. Not bothering to wipe off the stickiness, she turned to run. But a door banging and fearsome shouting forced her to cower back next to the poinsettia bush and freeze.

'*Jou bliksem! Ek sal jou moer!*'

It could only be Jan Venter. Veronica's Afrikaans was not very good despite the lessons at school. But she knew Meneer Venter was swearing and that 'moer' was 'murder'. Who was he going to murder now? Was she not perhaps already standing on his wife?

The commotion got worse. She could hear sounds of running and other people coming outside. An elderly woman in housemaid's uniform hurried down steps from the stoep close by to Veronica, without noticing her huddled against the wall. She was moaning softly to herself. Meneer Venter was shouting about people who stole from him. Everyone would see now what he did to thieves.

Veronica was trembling but she had to find out what was happening. She stretched forward to see around the corner. A small number of servants stood at a short distance from the massive figure—his face just a shade lighter than his blazing beard and hair. In front of him stood a black child with thin spindly legs, wearing a pair of torn khaki shorts, his eyes fixed on the ground. The man grabbed the boy's ear and jerked his head upwards, with his other hand forcing an orange into the boy's face.

'*Kyk hierso!* Look at this! I'll teach you a lesson you'll never forget!'

'Please Baas, this boy has learnt his lesson. He won't do it again Baas. I will speak to him Baas!'

It was the old housemaid, her hands together as if in a prayer, pleading, moving nearer to Meneer Venter. His arm swept out, dismissing her.

'He must learn a proper lesson. Talking is not good enough!'

The old woman was insistent. 'He's only a child, my Baas. Once the Baas was also a child!'

Meneer Venter turned on her now. 'You go too far now Lettie. Watch out or I'll give you a lesson too!'

The old woman covered her face with her hands, shaking her head.

Meneer Venter shouted instructions to a couple of servants who disappeared through the side door. One came back with a wooden chair and the other with a cane. For a moment after his ear had been released, the boy looked around wildly. In the second that Veronica glimpsed his eyes, she almost called out. He looked like Selo! Rebecca's son, in the photograph. It couldn't be him, could it? Rebecca's family lived far away. But Rebecca had said Selo was always getting into trouble.

The boy was ordered to lean over the chair. One of the male workers was ordered to stand in front and hold him down. Meneer Venter took the cane. Veronica did not look after the first two strikes. The boy's cries pierced her ears. She was shivering all over. Her stomach heaved.

When the cries reduced to a soft whimpering, Veronica looked up. To her horror, Meneer Venter was walking in her direction in a slow swagger. There was no time and nowhere to run. Standing transfixed, she dropped the flower in her hand. His eyes were odd, glazed, as if not seeing anything. Then, as he drew close, they flickered.

'*Jy is 'n van Reenen, nè?* Tell your father I'm satisfied with the fence.'

Before Veronica could even think what to say, he patted her hair lightly and walked on, up the steps and into the house. He had thought she was Marika.

Guiltily, Veronica looked down at the fallen poinsettia. She was aware of the old woman gently holding the boy, making soothing noises. The servants were talking quietly amongst themselves. Hastily she picked up the blood-red flower. The milky oozing had stopped and sealed up the stem. Grabbing a branch above her, she snapped off four more stems, careless of the sticky sap. A flower each. Sprinting down the road, she passed the old woman and the boy who had begun making their way painfully towards the huts behind the bluegums. No sounds followed as she entered the orange trees. She stopped running. She could walk the rest of the way now and give herself time to regain her breath. Then she could present each flower quite calmly. She might even take the gang some oranges.

A Minikin-Eared Ewe

Tsendyin Damdinsüren

By the age of thirteen, I had learned to drive sheep pretty well. Ready to move at any time of day or night, I pastured almost five hundred sheep belonging to our family and our neighbour for a whole six months. To be honest, by the end of that time I had become quite fed up with this work. As I drove my sheep through a lonely field, from sunrise to sunset, I could not find anyone to talk to. The only thing I longed for was the call to go home and have hot tea and curd.

I came to know my pasturing sheep quite well. I even got to know which sheep ate lizards, which sheep led the herd and ate the most nourishing grasses, and which lazy ones were the last to move. It is said that the sheep is a friendly, gregarious creature, but I soon realized that no such amiable nature existed. One sheep would eat aromatic grass just as another was about to feed on it. There is no such camaraderie among sheep as you find among horses. Being a clever animal, a horse not only becomes a man's close friend but also makes friends with its fellows. Among the horses are found friends, acquaintances and even enemies. No such relationships exist between sheep. Nonetheless, occasionally a reasonable one is to be found among them.

I once had an ewe with minikin (tiny) ears, a gift from my uncle on Tsagaan Star.[2] She was a clever sheep, and we were always on friendly terms. Whenever I called my minikin-eared ewe she would come to me from wherever she was in the flock. Eventually she began coming to me without my calling, and ended up following me everywhere. I always shared with her the food which my mother put in my pocket in the morning when I left home. She was very fond of sweets. It is true that cows do not like the taste of sweets, but sheep do. Whenever I gave a round piece of candy to my minikin-eared ewe, she would follow me the whole day, bleating for more.

One autumn, our two families had to move to a new place. Riding my slow grey pony, I began to herd the flock of sheep, intending to reach the new grazing ground before dusk. It was autumn, the season for fattening the sheep, so it was impossible to drive them fast.

My minikin-eared ewe came running up to me. I gave here a piece of sugar. As we drove forward our ger[3] in the new place came into sight. Since I had a faint idea of where we would be setting in, I reached it in a short time. The new country was a rich grassland with thick, tall and nutritious grass waving

---

[2] The New Year on the lunar calendar.
[3] A Mongolian dome-shaped house.

in the breeze. Although it appeared a little dried by the sun, it was much better than the grass in the old place. This new country had many small mounds and hillocks, every one of them covered with thick grass which looked like a fluffy fox cap. The grassy field ended only a few kilometres to the south of our ger, and then the landscape changed into gobi[4] and toirom[5] with red budargana[6] and yellow sagebrush. Animals love these bitter, salty plants. The contrast between the yellow field and the chestnut toirom made a strikingly beautiful scene.

When I brought my flock of sheep close to our ger, they were soon eagerly nibbling the rich juicy grass, never pausing to lift a head. On reaching my ger, I hitched my horse to a nearby cart and then scanned the horizon. Beneath the sinking sun, a thick dark cloud had gathered, and I said to myself, 'Heavy rain tomorrow,' then entered my ger.

As I sat drinking a cup of tea, someone outside suddenly yelled, 'Fire! Fire!' The voice belonged to the horseherd Avir.

When the three of us—my father, my mother and myself—ran out of the ger, the sun appeared like a blackened red disc. The wind was blowing from the west and we could smell the black smoke!

'There is a fire, and it is approaching. I saw flames from the top of a high mound. The fire is coming nearer!' gasped Avir, greatly troubled.

---

[4]Gobi Desert occupying 500,000 square miles in east-central Asia mostly in Mongolia.

[5]A dry circular salt marsh without vegetation and covered with crevices.

[6]Svaeda prostrata—a kind of plant.

My father and Avir tied some pieces of smoke-yellowed felts to the ends of long poles and rode towards the fire after wetting them. My mother harnessed a cow to a cart with a water barrel on it, and hurried after father and Avir. They were to fight the fire with those wet yellow felts, dipping them into the water barrel when they dried. As mother left, she called out 'Keep watch over the sheep!' Why should she say that? It appeared that there was no need to pay much attention to the sheep, for they were grazing peacefully around the gers. Anyhow, if the fire approached the gers, how could I alone look after all these sheep?

I stood motionless, simply wondering what my mother and father were doing at the time. If the wind is gentle and the grass sparse, fire can be easily extinguished by the wet felt. I was thinking of a similar incident that had happened once before.

The previous spring I had been playing on the open steppe with two other children. We built a little fire which soon spread to the dry spring grass, and suddenly there was a fire. Luckily the wind was not strong, and we managed to beat out the fire with our fur hats. That evening we caught it from our parents, for we had nearly started a steppe fire, and our fur hats had become like frizzled shanks. This fire, however, was different, for now the wind was strong and the grass was thick and dry.

Suddenly I realized I had no time to ponder over such things. I had to think of something quickly, and I looked around anxiously. Avir's mother, although an old lady, had lost no time. She had already cut the old dry grass growing near her ger, and was now clearing the grass around our ger.

We had several folding wooden pens for our sheep, but they were still lying on the carts. The old lady told me that it wouldn't be a bad idea to unload and erect them. True enough, if I could herd the sheep into the pens, maybe the fire would not harm them, so I quickly got to work. However hard I tried, though, I could not unload the fences to erect the pen, and the roaring fire had already reached us. The fire had crossed the western hillock, burning the grass to cinders. In the midst of the black smoke and leaping flames, I saw several horses running away at full speed. It was impossible to tell whose horses they were. Further away, a herd of antelopes was also seen running, and among them I thought I saw a pack of wolves. United by their mutual fear of fire, the wolves and antelopes were fleeing from it in one pack. Our sheep also began to panic as the flame and smoke drew closer. I mounted my poor grey horse to round up my scattered sheep.

The old people used to say that gazelles and antelopes fleeing to save themselves from fire in open country panic and lose strength. Even though the antelopes are fast runners, they get exhausted and, overtaken by the flames, are virtually burnt to death. Aflame and running, they then catch up with the other tired antelopes and set them on fire, as well.

The elders taught that one must never run away from a fire, but rather should go against it and get through the fire line. When you are standing on its ashes, the danger of the fire will have passed.

I resolved to collect my sheep and drive them against the fire to get them behind the fire line. The fire had burnt everything on the west, and was advancing eastward. The whole steppe was covered with leaping red flames and black smoke. Although the situation was now very serious and frightening, I called forth my courage, determined to defend my sheep. Mother had told me to look after all these sheep. I had to get them safely away from the fire by any possible means. The wind was quite strong. I hoped the flames would pass quickly, and thought that if I could keep my sheep gathered in one place, I might as well save them.

The blazing wall of flames approached our ger. I thought of asking Avir's mother what to do, but I saw her standing with her beloved dog on the cart with iron wheels. Therefore, the life of all these sheep depended entirely upon me.

During this frightening moment, the idea came to me to find my minikin-eared ewe and give her to the old woman. However, there was no time for that. The fire reached the cleared ground near our ger, and passed by the ger and the carts. Red flames raged high everywhere.

This sight encouraged me. As the fire was passing so quickly, I thought I could take my sheep to safety without having their wool catch fire. The only thing I had to do was to gather them and keep them together tightly in one place. That, I discovered, was impossible.

The sheep fled as soon as the fire came closer. I raced my horse before the sheep to collect them. Terrified of the fire, my lazy grey had become a swift grey. Her usual laziness was clearly wilful, for she now galloped wherever my reins demanded. Thanks to her I managed to prevent the sheep from scattering further.

However, my efforts were of little good to the sheep, for matters took their own course. Although I held the sheep from scattering, the fire had already begun to singe their fleece. Everywhere old dry grass was burning and my sheep looked as if they were on fire.

My horse galloped madly and I shouted until my lungs nearly burst, trying to drive the sheep against the fire. Despite my frantic efforts, I managed to take only about a hundred of them across the main fire line. The fire passed quickly, and I was left on the ashes with about a hundred sheep; a hundred fire-scorched sheep flocked together. Most of the sheep had run away with the fire, engulfed in flames and smoke. Leaving my hundred scorched sheep, I rode after the fire. Many sheep had been burnt black and lay helpless on the path. Usually the leg tendons of a sheep burn and shrink before anything else, causing the running animal to fall like a chopped tree. The numbers of such fallen sheep increased as my horse and I moved onward.

Suddenly, an idea struck me. If the few leading sheep were still unburnt, I could drive them into a salt marsh full of bundargana. Though a little late in coming, this wasn't such a bad idea, for the red bundargana in the salt marsh would not burn easily. In there, they would be safe.

I crossed the fire on my horse and, true enough, the sheep in the lead were fleeing unscorched. I separated over a hundred sheep from the flock and urged them on faster.

Then I saw that the level land ended in a deep valley filled with bundargana. Tall, thick straw grew in the hollow, and straw, I knew, burns easily. I had to drive my sheep through that straw before they caught fire, but as the straws were tall and dense, my sheep could not penetrate them. They came to a standstill. I struggled to get them out through the straw, and I and my horse managed to reach the edge of the dry circular salt marsh in time. Now there was no doubt whatsoever that very soon only the sheep's carcasses would be left. The tall, thick straw started burning with flames as high as two metres, and in the midst of that I knew that our sheep were burning. Thus, our sheep were annihilated.

My dear minikin-eared ewe was also probably burnt to death, but, I thought, she just may still be alive. I started calling with all my might, 'My minikin! My minikin! My minikin ewe, come out here!'

Then, a sheep came running out of the burning straw. It was my minikin-eared ewe. My ewe with the tiny ears! She wasn't at all harmed by the fire and had come at my calling. I was so relieved.

I hastily dismounted from my horse and kissed the ewe. She began rubbing my hands with her pretty soft muzzle, asking for a candy, as if everything around was calm and peaceful. Hearing my voice she had perhaps thought that I was going to give her some candies. This thought had saved her life.

Following the minikin-eared ewe, ten sheep came out of the burning straw. As anyone knows, sheep always follow where the others go. The ten sheep that were closest to the ewe had come out of the straws, but the rest were burnt to death. I saw with my own eyes many sheep burning alive in the straws. The fire burnt the straws in the hollow land, but died down when it reached the dry circular salt marsh bundargana. I was safe from danger, and so was my minikin-eared ewe.

Only charred carcasses were left of several hundred sheep which I had herded for so long. As I drove the remaining ten sheep with my minikin-eared ewe back toward home, I saw burning dry dung, rising smoke and half-burnt sheep struggling and dying.

Darkness had already fallen when I arrived home. Although my parents were very glad to see me alive and safe, I felt so depressed as I recalled my mother's words, 'Keep watch over the sheep!'

The hundred sheep which I had taken through the fire were flocked together near the ger. I let the ten sheep and the ewe join them. They were all that remained of the hundreds of sheep that we had owned.

The next day I searched for our horses, and found them in the bundargana-filled ravine. They had run into the ravine and so were safe and sound, out of danger of the fire.

Our neighbour Tavkhai's sheep were not at all harmed by the fire, for he had locked them in a pen. I regretted bitterly not having been able to either erect a pen around my sheep or do drive them into the ravine with bundargana. This time, however, I had erred by following the older people's instructions to drive the sheep against the fire. I reminded myself to enter a ravine with bundargana if anything like this should happen again. My parents should not have left me alone with so many sheep as they left to fight the fire. When one thinks over mistakes afterwards, their causes become more clear.

The day after the fire was put out, our family moved to a new place. We chose ten to twenty fat sheep from among the dead ones, and we invited the local people to choose any of the remaining sheep. Because it was a warm autumn day, the carcasses were liable to rot quickly.

As we migrated, the country where just a few days before fine dry grass had been swaying now looked like a barren wasteland. It had a ghastly, dead look. The fine dry grass of the pasture land had become loose grey ash-strewn everywhere one looked.

A great deal of livestock and property belonging to many families was lost or ruined in this fire. If there hadn't been that ravine with bundargana nearby, the fire would have progressed farther, bringing much more damage and sorrow. Disasters of this kind sometimes break out in the steppes, leaving behind complete desolation.

Later I heard the following report: The fire started near the Gerel family, people said. Gerel's two sons used to smoke while they tended their sheep. They never had matches, so they always had dry dung burning. This time their burning dung had been scattered in the strong wind, and fire had broken out in the grass. The two boys became confused, and in fear ran away instead of attempting to put out the fire. The fire then raged wildly, destroying entire neighbouring pastures until it reached the ravine with bundargana, where it finally died out.

Once again I tended the sheep which were left alive. The poor sheep, burnt and scorched, were feeding about me. Among them my dear minikin-eared ewe was the whitest of all, and was still on such friendly terms with me. At first, the sheep appeared to me only a little singed, apparently without having come to much harm, but as winter approached, the hooves of the injured sheep fell off and many died. In spring several ewes had lambed, but they could not feed their lambs, for their nipples had been burnt in the fire, so our flock of sheep born in spring was decreased even further. Happily, my minikin-eared ewe had given birth to two fine lambs, also with tiny ears, and they were growing quite well.

Years passed, and I became a man of the city. One summer I returned to my family's ger in the country. Seeing many sheep with minikin ears among our flock of sheep, I recalled my dear minikin-eared ewe and the disastrous fire.

'These sheep with tiny ears are probably the off-springs of my ewe with minikin ears,' I thought. Since that time, I have had a special liking to any ewe with minikin ears.

Translated by D. Altangerel

Valia

Leonid Andreiev

VALIA WAS reading a huge, very huge book, almost half as large as himself, with very black letters and pictures occupying the entire page. To see the top line Valia had to stretch out his neck, lean far over the table, kneeling in his chair, and putting his short chubby ringer on the letters for fear they would be lost among the other ones like it, in which case it was a difficult task to find them again. Owing to these circumstances, unforeseen by the publishers, the reading advanced very slowly, notwithstanding the breath-catching interest of the book.

It was a story about a very strong boy whose name was Prince Bova, and who could, by merely grasping the legs or arms of other boys, wrench them away from the body.

But Valia was suddenly interrupted in his reading; his mother entered with some other woman.

'Here he is,' said his mother, her eyes red with weeping.

The tears had evidently been shed very recently as she was still crushing a white lace handkerchief in her hand.

'Valichka, darling!' exclaimed the other woman, and putting her arms about his head, she began to kiss his face and eyes, pressing her thin, hard lips to them. She did not fondle him as did his mother, whose kisses were soft and melting; this one seemed loath to let go of him. Valia accepted her pricking caresses with a frown and silence; he was very much displeased at being interrupted, and he did not at all like this strange woman, tall, with bony, long fingers upon which there was not even one ring. And she smelled so bad: a damp, mouldy smell, while his mother always exhaled a fresh, exquisite perfume.

At last the woman left him in peace, and while he was wiping his lips she looked him over with that quick sort of glance which seemed to photograph one. His short nose with its indication of a future little hump, his thick, unchildish brows over dark eyes, and the general appearance of stern seriousness, recalled someone to her, and she began to cry. Even her weeping was unlike mama's: the face remained immovable while the tears quickly rolled down one after the other before one had time to fall another was already chasing after it. Her tears ceased as suddenly as they had commenced, and she asked, 'Valichka, do you know me?' 'No.'

'I called to see you. Twice I called to see you.'

Perhaps she had called upon him, perhaps she had called twice, but how should Valia know of it? With her questions she only hindered him from reading.

'I am your mama, Valia!' said the woman.

Valia looked around in astonishment to find his mama, but she was no longer in the room.

'Why, can there be two mamas?' he asked. 'What nonsense you are telling me?'

The woman laughed, but this laugh did not please Valia; it was evident that the woman did not wish to laugh at all, and did it purposely to fool him. For some moments they were both silent.

'And what book is it you are reading?'

'About Prince Bova,' Valia informed her with serious self-esteem and an evident respect for the big book.

'Ach, it must be very interesting! Tell me, please!' the woman asked with an ingratiating smile.

And once more something unnatural and false sounded in this voice, which tried to be soft and round like the voice of his mother, but remained sharp and prickly. The same insincerity appeared also in all the movements of the woman; she turned on her chair and even stretched out her neck with a manner as if preparing for a long and attentive listening; and when Valia reluctantly began the story, she immediately retired within herself like a dark lantern on which the cover is suddenly thrown. Valia felt the offense toward himself and Prince Bova, but, wishing to be polite, he quickly finished the story and added, 'That is all.'

'Well, goodbye, my dear, my dove!' said the strange woman, and once more pressed her lips to Valia's face. 'I shall soon call again. Will you be glad?'

'Yes, come please,' politely replied Valia, and to get rid of her more quickly he added, 'I will be very glad.'

The visitor left him, but hardly had Valia found in the book again the word at which he had been interrupted, when mama entered, looked at him, and she also began to weep. He could easily understand why the other woman should have wept; she must have been sorry that she was so unpleasant and tiresome but why should his mama weep?

'Listen, mama,' he said musingly, 'how that woman bored me! She says that she is my mama. Why, could there be two mamas to one boy?'

'No, baby, there could not; but she speaks the truth; she is your mother.'

'And what are you, then?'

'I am your auntie.'

This was a very unexpected discovery, but Valia received it with unshakable indifference; auntie, well, let it be auntie was it not just the same? A word did not, as yet, have the same meaning for him as it would for a grown person. But his former mother did not understand it, and began to explain why it had so happened that she had been a mother and had become an aunt. Once, very long ago, when Valia was very, very little

'How little? So?' Valia raised his hand about a quarter of a yard from the table. 'Like Kiska?' Valia exclaimed, joyfully surprised, with mouth half opened and brow lifted. He spoke of his white kitten that had been presented to him.

'Yes.'

Valia broke into a happy laugh, but immediately resumed his usual earnestness, and with the condescension of a grown person recalling the mistakes of his youth, he remarked, 'How funny I must have been!'

When he was so very little and funny, like Kiska, he had been brought by that woman and given away forever, also like Kiska. And now, when he had become so big and clever, the woman wanted him.

'Do you wish to go to her?' asked his former mother and reddened with joy when Valia resolutely and sternly said, 'No, she does not please me!' and once more took up his book.

Valia considered the affair closed, but he was mistaken. This strange woman, with a face as devoid of life as if all the blood had been drained out of it, who had appeared from no one knew where, and vanished without leaving a trace, seemed to have set the whole house in turmoil and filled it with a dull alarm. Mama-auntie often cried and repeatedly asked Valia if he wished to leave her; uncle-papa grumbled, patted his bald pate so that the sparse, grey hair on it stood up, and when auntie-mama was absent from the room he also asked Valia if he would like to go to that woman. Once, in the evening, when Valia was already in his little bed but was not yet sleeping, he heard his uncle and auntie speaking of him and the woman. The uncle spoke in an angry basso at which the crystal pendants of the chandelier gently trembled and sparkled with bluish and reddish lights.

'You speak nonsense, Nastasia Philippovna. We have no right to give the child away.'

'She loves him, Grisha.'

'And we! Do we not love him? You are arguing very strangely, Nastasia Philippovna. It seems as if you would be glad to get rid of the child.'

'Are you not ashamed of yourself?'

'Well, well, how quick you are to take offense. Just consider this matter cold-bloodedly and reasonably. Some frivolous thing or other gives birth to children, light-heartedly disposes of them by placing them on your threshold, and afterward says, "Kindly give me my child, because, on account of my lover having abandoned me, I feel lonesome. For theatres and concerts I have no money, so give me the child to serve as a toy to play with." No, madam, be easy, we shall see who wins in this case!'

'You are unjust to her, Grisha. You know well how ill and lonely she is.'

'You, Nastasia Philippovna, can make even a saint lose patience, by God! And the child you seem to have forgotten? For you is it wholly immaterial whether he is brought up an honest man or a scoundrel? And I could bet my head that he would be brought up by her a rascal and scoundrel.'

'Grisha!'

'I ask you, for God's sake, not to irritate me! And where did you get this devilish habit of contradicting? "She is so lonely." And are we not lonely? The heartless woman that you are, Nastasia Philippovna! And why the devil did I marry you!'

The heartless woman broke into tears, and her husband immediately begged her pardon, declaring that only a born fool could pay any attention to the words of such an old ass as he was. Gradually she became calmer and asked, 'What does Talonsky say?'

'And what makes you think that he is such a clever fellow?' Gregory Aristarchovich again flew into a passion. 'He says that everything depends on how the court will look at it. Something new, is it not, as if we did not know without his telling that everything depends on how the court will look at it!' Of course it matters little to him, what does he care? He will have his bark and then he will safely go his way. If I had my way, it would go ill with all these empty talkers."

But here Nastasia Philippovna shut the dining room door and Valia did not hear the end of the conversation. But he lay for a long time with open eyes, trying to understand what sort of woman it was who wished to take him away from his home and ruin him.

On the next day he waited from early morning expecting his auntie to ask him if he wished to go to his mother; but auntie did not ask. Neither did his uncle. Instead of this, they both gazed at Valia as if he were dangerously ill and would soon die; they caressed him and brought him large books with coloured pictures. The woman did not call any more, but it seemed to Valia that she must be lurking outside the door watching for him, and that as soon as he would pass the threshold she would seize him and carry him out into a black and dismal distance where cruel monsters were wriggling and breathing fire.

In the evenings while his Uncle Gregory Aristarchovich was occupied in his study and Nastasia Philippovna was knitting something, or playing a game of solitaire, Valia read his books, in which the lines would grow gradually thicker and the letters smaller. Everything in the room was quiet, so quiet that the only thing to be heard was the rustling of the pages he turned, and occasionally the uncle's loud cough from the study, or the striking of the abacus counters. The lamp, with its blue shade, threw a bright light on the blue plush table cover, but the corners of the room were full of a quiet, mysterious gloom.

There stood large plants with curious leaves and roots crawling out upon the surface and looking very much like fighting serpents, and it seemed as if something large and dark was moving amidst them. Valia read, and before his wide-open eyes passed terrible, beautiful and sad images which awakened in him pity and love, but more often fear. Valia was sorry for the poor water-nymph who so dearly loved the handsome prince that for him she had given up her sisters and the deep, peaceful ocean; and the prince knew nothing of this love, because the poor water-nymph was dumb, and so he married a gay princess; and while great festivities in honour of the wedding were in full swing on board the ship, and music was playing and all were enjoying themselves, the poor water-nymph threw herself into the dark waves to die. Poor, sweet little water-nymph, so quiet and sad, and modest!

But often terrible, cruel, human monsters appeared before Valia. In the dark nights they flew somewhere on their prickly wings, and the air whistled over their heads, and their eyes burned like red-hot coals. And afterward, they were surrounded by other monsters like themselves while a mysterious and terrible something was happening there. Laughter as sharp as a knife, long and pitiful wailing; strange weird dances in the purplish light of torches, their slanty, fiery tongues wrapped in the red clouds of smoke; and dead men with long, black beards; all this was the manifestation of a single enigmatic and cruel power, wishing to destroy man. Angry and mysterious spectres filled the air, hid among the plants, whispered something, and pointed their bony fingers at Valia; they gazed at him from behind the door of the adjoining unlit room, giggled and waited till he would go to bed, when they would silently dart around over his head; they peeped at him from out of the garden through the large, dark windows, and wailed sorrowfully with the wind.

In and out among all this vicious and terrible throng appeared the image of that woman who had come for Valia. Many people came and went in the house of Gregory Aristarchovich, and Valia did not remember their faces, but this face lived in his memory. It was such an elongated, thin, yellow face, and smiled with a sly, dissembling smile, from which two deep lines appeared at the two corners of the mouth. If this woman took Valia he would die.

'Listen,' Valia once said to his aunt, tearing himself away from his book for a moment. 'Listen,' he repeated with his usual earnestness, and with a glance that gazed straight into the eyes of the person with whom he spoke, 'I shall call you mama, not auntie. You talk nonsense when you say that the woman is mama. You are mama, not she.'

'Why?' asked Nastasia Philippovna, blushing like a young girl who had just received a compliment. But along with her joy there could also be heard in her voice the sound of fear for Valia. He had become so strange of late, and timid; feared to sleep alone, as he used to do, raved in his sleep and cried.

'But, Valichka, it is true, she is your mother.'

'I really wonder where you get this habit of contradicting!'

Valia said after some musing, imitating the tone of Gregory Aristarchovich.

Nastasia Philippovna laughed, but while preparing for bed that night she spoke for a considerable time with her husband, who boomed like a Turkish drum, abused the empty talkers, and frivolous, hairbrained women, and afterwards went with his wife to see Valia.

They gazed long and silently into the face of the sleeping child. The flame of the candle swayed in the trembling hand of Gregory Aristarchovich and lent a fantastic, death-like colouring to the face of the boy, which was as white as the pillows on which it rested. It seemed as if a pair of stern, black eyes looked at them from the dark hollows, demanding a reply and threatening them with misfortune and unknown sorrow, and the lips twitched into a strange, ironic smile as if upon his helpless child-head lay a vague reflection of those cruel and mysterious spectre monsters that silently hovered over it.

'Valia!' whispered the frightened Nastasia. The boy sighed deeply but did not move, as if enchained in the sleep of death.

'Valia! Valia!' the deep, trembling voice of her husband was added to that of Nastasia Philippovna.

Valia opened his eyes, shaded by thick eyelashes; the light of the candle made him wink, and he sprang to his knees, pale and frightened. His uncovered, thin little arms, like a pearl necklace encircled his auntie's full, rosy neck, and hiding his little head upon her breast and screwing up his eyes tight as if fearing that they would open of themselves, he whispered, 'I am afraid, mama, I am afraid! Do not go!'

That was a bad night for the whole household; when Valia

at last fell asleep, Gregory Aristarchovich got an attack of asthma. He choked, and his full, white breast rose and fell spasmodically under the ice compresses. Toward morning he grew more tranquil, and the worn Nastasia fell asleep with the thought that her husband would not survive the loss of the child.

After a family council at which it was decided that Valia ought to read less and to see more of children of his own age, little girls and boys were brought to the house to play with him. But Valia from the first conceived a dislike for these foolish children who, in his eyes, were too noisy, loud and indecorous. They pulled flowers, tore books, jumped over chairs, and fought like little monkeys; and he, serious and thoughtful, looked on at their pranks with amazement and displeasure, and, going up to Nastasia Philippovna, said, 'They tire me! I would rather sit by you.' And in the evenings he once more took up his book, and when Gregory Aristarchovich, grumbling at all the deviltry the child read about, and by which he was losing his senses, gently tried to take the book from Valia's hands, the child silently and irresolutely pressed it to himself. And the improvised pedagogue beat a confused retreat and angrily scolded his wife:

'Is this what you call bringing up! No, Nastasia Philippovna, I see you are more fit to take care of kittens than to bring up children. The boy is so spoiled that one can not even take a book away from him.'

One morning while Valia was sitting at breakfast with Nastasia Philippovna, Gregory Aristarchovich suddenly came rushing into the dining room. His hat was tilted on the back of his head, his face was covered with perspiration; while still at the other side of the door he shouted joyfully into the room:

'Refused! The court has refused!'

The diamond earrings in Nastasia Philippovna's ears began to sparkle, and the little knife she held in her hand dropped to the plate.

'Is it true?' she asked, breathlessly.

Gregory Aristarchovich made a serious face, just to show that he had spoken the truth, but immediately forgetting his intention, his face became covered with a whole network of merry wrinkles. Then once more remembering that he lacked that earnestness of demeanour with which important news is usually imparted, he frowned, pushed a chair up to the table, placed his hat upon it, forgot that it was his hat, and thinking the chair to be already occupied by someone, threw a stern look at Nastasia Philippovna, then on Valia, winked his eye at Valia; and only after all these solemn preliminaries did he declare:

'I always said that Talonsky was a devilishly clever fellow; can't fool him easily, Nastasia Philippovna.'

'So it is true?'

'You are always ready with your eternal doubts. I said the case of Mme. Akimova is dismissed. Clever, is it not, little brother?' he turned to Valia and added in a stern, official tone: 'And that said Akimova is to pay the costs.'

'That woman will not take me, then?'

'I guess she won't, brother mine! Ach, I have entirely forgotten, I brought you some books!'

Gregory Aristarchovich rushed into the corridor, but

halted on hearing Nastasia Philippovna's scream. Valia had fallen back on his chair in a faint.

A happy time began for the family. It was as if some one who had lain dangerously ill in the house had suddenly recovered and all began to breathe more easily and freely. Valia lost his fear of the terrible monsters and no longer suffered from nightmares. When the little monkeys, as he called the children, came to see him again, he was the most inventive of the lot. But even into the most fantastic plays he introduced his habitual earnestness and staidness, and when they played Indians, he found it indispensable to divest himself of almost all his clothing and cover his body with red paint.

In view of the businesslike manner in which these games were conducted, Gregory Aristarchovich now found it possible to participate in them, as far as his abilities allowed. In the role of a bear he did not appear to great advantage, but he had a great and well-deserved success in his role of an elephant. And when Valia, silent and earnest as a true son of the Goddess Kali, sat upon his father's shoulders and gently tapped upon his rosy bald pate with a tiny toy hammer, he really reminded one of a little Eastern prince who despotically reigns over people and animals.

The lawyer Talonsky tried to convey a hint to Gregory Aristarchovich that all was not safe yet, but the former could not comprehend how three judges could reverse the decision of three other judges, when the laws are the same here and everywhere. And when the lawyer insisted, Gregory Aristarchovich grew angry, and to prove that there was nothing to be feared from the higher court, he brought forward that same Talonsky on whom he now implicitly relied:

'Why, are you not going to be present when the case is brought before the court? Well, then what is there to be talked about. I wish you, Nastasia Philippovna, would make him ashamed of himself.'

Talonsky smiled, and Nastasia Philippovna gently chided him for his purposeless doubts. They also spoke of the woman who had caused all the trouble, but now that she could menace them no more, and the court had decided that she must bear all the costs of the trial, they often dubbed her 'poor woman.'

Since the day Valia had heard that the woman had no longer any power to take him, she had lost in his eyes the halo of mysterious fear, which enveloped her like a mist and distorted the features of her thin face, and Valia began to think of her as he did of all other people. He now repeatedly heard that she was unhappy and could not understand why; but her pale bloodless face grew more simple, natural and near to him, the 'poor woman,' as they called her, began to interest him, and recalling other poor women of whom he had read, he felt a growing pity and a timid tenderness for her.

He imagined that she must sit alone in some dark room, fearing something and weeping, always weeping, as she had wept when she had come to see him. And he felt sorry that he had not told her the story of Prince Bova better than he had at the time.

It appeared that three judges could, after all, disagree with the decision of three other judges. The higher court had reversed the decision of the district court, the child was adjudged to his real mother. And the appeal was not considered by the senate.

When the woman came to take Valia away with her, Gregory Aristarchovich was not at home, he was at Talonsky's house and was lying in Talonsky's bedroom, and only the bald, rosy pate was visible above the sea of snow-white pillows.

Nastasia Philippovna did not leave her room, and the maid led Valia forth from it already dressed for the road. He wore a fur coat and tall overshoes in which he moved his feet with difficulty. From under his fur cap looked out a pale little face with a frank and serious expression in the dark eyes. Under his arm Valia carried a book in which was the story of a poor water-nymph.

The tall, gaunt woman pressed the boy to her shabby coat and sobbed out, 'How you have grown, Valichka! You are unrecognizable,' she said, trying to joke, but Valia adjusted his cap and, contrary to habit, did not look into the eyes of the one who from this day on was to be his mother, but into her mouth. It was large, but with beautiful, small teeth; the two wrinkles on the corners of the mouth were still on the same place where Valia had seen them first, only now they were deeper.

'You are not angry with me?' asked mama; but Valia, not replying to her question, said: 'Let us be gone.'

'Valichka!' came a pitiful scream from Nastasia Philippovna's room, and she appeared on the threshold with eyes swollen from weeping, and clasping her hands she rushed toward the child, sank on her knees, and put her head on his shoulder. She did not utter a sound, only the diamonds in her ears trembled.

'Come, Valia,' sternly said the tall woman, taking his hand. 'We must not remain any longer among people who have subjected your mother to such torture—such torture!'

Her dry voice was full of hatred and she longed to strike the kneeling woman with her foot.

'Ugh! Heartless wretches! You would be glad to take even my only child from me!' she wrathfully whispered, and pulled Valia away by his hand. 'Come! Don't be like your father, who abandoned me.'

'Ta-ke ca-re of him,' Nastasia called after them.

The hired sleigh which stood waiting for them flew softly and lightly over the snow and noiselessly carried Valia away from the quiet house with its wonderful plants and flowers, its mysterious fairy tale world, immeasurable and deep as the sea, with its windows gently screened by the boughs of the tall trees of the garden. Soon the house was lost in the mass of other houses, as similar to each other as the letters in Valia's book, and vanished forever from Valia.

It seemed to him as if they were swimming in a river, the banks of which were constituted of rows of lanterns as close to each other as beads on a string, but when they approached nearer, the beads were scattered, forming large, dark spaces and merging behind into just such a line of light. And then Valia thought that they were standing motionless on the very same spot; and everything began to be like a fairy tale he himself and the tall woman who was pressing him to her with her bony hand, and everything around him.

The hand in which he carried his book was getting stiff with cold, but he would not ask his mother to take the book from him.

The small room into which Valia's mother had taken him was untidy and hot; in a corner near the large bed stood a little curtained bed such as Valia had not slept in for a long, long time.

'You are frozen! Well, wait, we shall soon have some tea! Well, now you are with your mama. Are you glad?' his mother asked with the hard, unpleasant look of one who has been forced to smile beneath blows all her life long.

'No,' Valia replied shyly, frightened at his own frankness.

'No? And I had bought some toys for you. Just look, there they are on the window.'

Valia approached the window and examined the toys. They were wretched paper horses with straight, thick legs, Punch with a red cap on, with an idiotically grinning face and a large nose, and little tin soldiers with one foot raised in the air.

Valia had long ago given up playing with toys and did not like them, but from politeness he did not show it to his mother. 'Yes, they are nice toys,' he said.

She noticed the glance he threw at the window, and said with that unpleasant, ingratiating smile, 'I did not know what you liked, darling, and I bought them for you a long time ago.'

Valia was silent, not knowing what to reply.

'You must know that I am all alone, Valia, all alone in the wide world; I have no one whose advice I could ask; I thought they would please you.' Valia was silent.

Suddenly the muscles of the woman's face relaxed and the tears began to drop from her eyes, quickly, quickly, one after the other; and she threw herself on the bed which gave a pitiful squeak under the weight of her body, and with one hand pressed to her breast, the other to her temples, she looked vacantly through the wall with her pale, faded eyes, and whispered,

'He was not pleased! Not pleased!'

Valia promptly approached the bed, put his little hand, still red with the cold, on the large head of his mother, and spoke with the same serious staidness which distinguished this boy's speech,

'Do not cry, mama. I will love you very much. I do not care to play with toys, but I will love you ever so much. If you wish, I will read to you the story of the poor water-nymph.'

Translated by Lizzie B. Gorin

The Accursed House

Emile Gaboriau

The Vicomte de B_____, an amiable and charming young man, was peacefully enjoying an income of 30,000 livres yearly, when, unfortunately for him, his uncle, a miser of the worst species, died, leaving him all his wealth, amounting to nearly two millions.

In running through the documents of succession, the Vicomte de B_____ learned that he was the proprietor of a house in the Rue de la Victoire. He learned, also, that the unfurnished building, bought in 1849 for 300,000 francs, now brought in, clear of taxes, rentals amounting to 82,000 francs a year.

'Too much, too much, entirely,' thought the generous vicomte, 'my uncle was too hard; to rent at this price is usury, one cannot deny it. When one bears a great name like mine, one should not lend himself to such plundering. I will begin tomorrow to lower my rents, and my tenants will bless me.'

With this excellent purpose in view, the Vicomte de B_____ sent immediately for the *concièrge* of the building, who presented himself as promptly, with back bent like a bow.

'Bernard, my friend,' said the vicomte, 'go at once from me and notify all your tenants that I lower their rents by one-third.'

That unheard-of word 'lower' fell like a brick on Bernard's head. But he quickly recovered himself; he had heard badly; he had not understood.

'Low—er the rents!' stammered he. 'Monsieur le Vicomte deigns to jest. Lower! Monsieur, of course means to raise the rents.'

'I was never more serious in my life, my friend,' the vicomte returned; 'I said, and I repeat it, lower the rents.'

This time the *concièrge* was surprised to the point of bewilderment—so thrown off his balance that he forgot himself and lost all restraint.

'Monsieur has not reflected,' persisted he. 'Monsieur will regret this evening. Lower the tenants' rents! Never was such a thing known, monsieur! If the lodgers should learn of it, what would they think of monsieur? What would people say in the neighbourhood? Truly—'

'Monsieur Bernard, my friend,' dryly interrupted the vicomte, 'I prefer, when I give an order, to be obeyed without reply. You hear me—go!'

Staggering like a drunken man, Monsieur Bernard went out from the house of his proprietor.

All his ideas were upset, overthrown, confounded. Was he, or was he not, the plaything of a dream, a ridiculous nightmare? Was he himself Pierre Bernard, or Bernard somebody else?

'Lower his rents! Lower his rents!' repeated he. 'It is not to be believed! If indeed the lodgers had complained! But they have not complained; on the contrary, all are good payers. Ah! If his uncle could only know this, he would rise from the tomb! His nephew has gone mad, 'tis certain! Lower the rents! They should have this young man before a family council; he will finish badly! Who knows—after this—what he will do next? He lunched too well, perhaps, this morning.'

And the worthy Bernard was so pale with emotion when he re-entered his lodge, so pale and spent, that on seeing him enter, his wife and daughter Amanda exclaimed as with one voice:

'Goodness! What is it? What has happened to you now?'

'Nothing,' responded he, with altered voice, 'absolutely nothing.'

'You are deceiving me,' insisted Madame Bernard, 'you are concealing something from me; do not spare me; speak, I am strong—what did the new proprietor tell you? Does he think of turning us off?'

'If it were only that! But just think, he told me with his own lips, he told me to—ah! You will never believe me—'

'Oh, yes; only do go on.'

'You will have it, then!—Well, then, he told me, he ordered me to notify all the tenants that—*he lowered their rents one-third*! Did you hear what I said? —*lowered* the rents of the tenants—'

But neither Madame nor Mademoiselle Bernard heard

him out—they were twisting and doubling with convulsive laughter.

'Lower!' repeated they; 'ah! What a good joke, what a droll man! Lower the tenants' rents.'

But Bernard, losing his temper and insisting that he must be taken seriously in his own lodge, his wife lost her temper too, and a quarrel followed! Madame Bernard declaring that Monsieur Bernard had, beyond a doubt, taken his fantastic order from the bottom of a litre of wine in the restaurant at the corner.

But for Mademoiselle Amanda the couple would undoubtedly have come to blows, and finally Madame Bernard, who did not wish to be thought demented, threw a shawl over her head and ran to the proprietor's house. Bernard had spoken truly; with her own two ears, ornamented with big, gilded hoops, she heard the incredible word. Only, as she was a wise and prudent woman, she demanded 'a bit of writing' to put, as she said, 'her responsibility under cover.'

She, too, returned thunderstruck, and all the evening in the lodge, father, mother, and daughter deliberated.

Should they obey? Or should they warn some relative of this mad young man, whose common sense would oppose itself to such insanity?

They decided to obey.

Next morning, Bernard, buttoning himself into his best frock coat, made the rounds of the three-and-twenty lodges to announce his great news.

Ten minutes afterward the house in the Rue de la Victoire was in a state of commotion impossible to describe. People who, for forty years had lived on the same floor, and never honoured each other with so much as a tip of the hat, now clustered together and chatted eagerly.

'Do you know, monsieur?'

'It is very extraordinary.'

'Simply unheard of!'

'The proprietor's lowered my rent!'

'One-third, is it not? Mine also.'

'Astounding! It *must* be a mistake!'

And despite the affirmations of the Bernard family, despite even the 'bit of writing' 'under cover,' there were found among the tenants doubting Thomases, who doubted still in the face of everything.

Three of them actually wrote to the proprietor to tell him what had passed, and to charitably warn him that his *concièrge* had wholly lost his mind. The proprietor responded to these skeptics, confirming what Bernard had said. Doubt, thereafter, was out of the question.

Then began reflections and commentaries.

'*Why* had the proprietor lowered his rents?'

'Yes, *why*?'

'What motives,' said they all, 'actuate this strange man? For certainly he must have grave reasons for a step like this! An intelligent man, a man of good sense, would never deprive himself of good fat revenues, well secured, for the simple pleasure of depriving himself. One would not conduct himself thus without being forced, constrained by powerful or terrible circumstances.'

And each said to himself:

'*There is something under all this!*'

'But what?'

And from the first floor to the sixth they sought and conjectured and delved in their brains. Every lodger had the preoccupied air of a man that strives with all his wits to solve an impossible cipher, and everywhere there began to be a vague disquiet, as it happens when one finds himself in the presence of a sinister mystery.

Someone went so far as to hazard, 'This man must have committed a great and still hidden crime; remorse pushes him to philanthropy.'

'It was not a pleasant idea, either, the thought of living thus side by side with a rascal; no, by no means; he might be repentant, and all that, but suppose he yielded to temptation once more!'

'The house, perhaps, was badly built?' questioned another, anxiously.

'Hum-m, so-so! No one could tell; but all knew one thing—it was very, very old!'

'True! And it had been necessary to prop it when they dug the drain last year in the month of March.'

'Maybe it was the roof, then, and the house is top-heavy?' suggested a tenant on the fifth floor.

'Or perhaps,' said a lodger in the garret, 'there is a press for coining counterfeit money in the cellar; I have often heard at night a sound like the dull, muffled thud of a coin-stamper.'

The opinion of another was that Russian, maybe Prussian, spies had gained a lodgment in the house, while the gentleman of the first story was inclined to believe that the proprietor purposed to set fire to his house and furniture with the sole object of drawing great sums from the insurance companies.

Then began to happen, as they all declared, extraordinary and even frightful things. On the sixth and mansard floors it appeared that strange and absolutely inexplicable noises were heard. Then the nurse of the old lady on the fourth floor, going one night to steal wine from the cellar, encountered the ghost of the defunct proprietor—he even held in his hand a receipt for rent—by which she knew him!

And the refrain from loft to cellar was:

'There is something under all this!'

From disquietude it had come to fright; from fright it quickly passed to terror. So that the gentleman of the first floor, who had valuables in his rooms, made up his mind to go, and sent in notice by his clerk.

Bernard went to inform the proprietor, who responded:

'All right, let the fool go!'

But next day the chiropodist of the second floor, though he had naught to fear for his valuables, imitated the gentleman beneath him. Then the bachelors and the little households of the fifth story quickly followed this example.

From that moment it was a general rout. By the end of the week, everybody had given notice. Every one awaited some frightful catastrophe. They slept no more. They organized patrols. The terrified domestics swore that they too would quit the accursed house and remained temporarily only on tripled wages.

Bernard was no more than the ghost of himself; the fever of fear had worn him to a shadow.

'No,' repeated his wife mournfully at each fresh notification, 'no, it is not natural.'

Meanwhile three-and-twenty 'For Rent' placards swung against the facade of the house, drawing an occasional applicant for lodgings.

Bernard—never grumbling now—climbed the staircase and ushered the visitor from apartment to apartment.

'You can have your choice,' said he to the people that presented themselves, 'the house is entirely vacant; all the tenants have given notice as one man. They do not know why, exactly, but *things* have happened, oh! yes, things! A mystery such as was never before known—*the proprietor has lowered his rents*!'

And the would-be lodgers fled away affrighted.

The term ended, three-and-twenty vans carried away the furniture of the three-and-twenty tenants. Everybody left. From top to bottom, from foundations to garret, the house lay empty of lodgers.

The rats themselves, finding nothing to live on, abandoned it also.

Only the *concièrge* remained, grey green with fear in his lodge. Frightful visions haunted his sleep. He seemed to hear lugubrious howlings and sinister murmurs at night that made his teeth chatter with terror and his hair erect itself under his cotton nightcap. Madame Bernard no more closed an eye than he. And Amanda in her frenzy renounced all thought of the operatic stage and married—for nothing in the world but to quit the paternal lodge—a young barber and hair-dresser whom she had never before been able to abide.

At last, one morning, after a more frightful nightmare than usual, Bernard, too, took a great resolution. He went to the proprietor, gave up his keys, and scampered away.

And now on the Rue de la Victoire stands the abandoned house, 'The Accursed House,' whose history I have told you. Dust thickens upon the closed flats, grass grows in the court. No tenant ever presents himself now; and in the quarter, where stands this Accursed House, so funereal is its reputation that even the neighbouring houses on either side of it have also depreciated in value.

Lower one's rents!! Who would think of such a thing!!

Translated by E.C. Waggener

Saritha Kamakshi Makes a Mistake

Jerry Pinto

*T*HAT EVENING *when Mr Swami returned home, Mrs Swami took one look at him and went to the fridge. She took out an earthen pot and spooned four huge blobs of curd into a dish.*

'Before that,' said Mr Swami weakly, 'one cup of coffee, please.'

'You will stay up all night, Kumar,' said Mrs Swami. 'Instead I will give you a glass of rasam and then you will have some tair-shaadam. After that you will tell me what has happened.'

Mr Swami acquiesced. Many years of being married to Saritha Kamakshi had made him realize that if she did not want him to have coffee, he would not get coffee. He waited as she heated some rasam and added two leaves of fresh tulsi and two fresh curry leaves. He drank it down and chewed the leaves and did feel somewhat better. He did not say this, but he suspected that Saritha Kamakshi knew.

'So what happened?'

'Today Adityasaahab bought the house.'

'*From that Parsi fellow?*'

'*From him only. The cheque was also given.*'

'*Good, good.*'

Adityasaahab was the son of one of the wealthiest men in India, but he was also the kind who could not give anyone a cheque without feeling physical pain. So he had waited until he got one more month's interest from the bank. Naturally, he had not told this to Mr Billimoria, the owner of the beautiful old bungalow that he was in the process of buying.

But Mr Billimoria had guessed. He had called up every day after the last date to ask when the cheque would be ready. It had been Mr Swami's duty to tell Mr Billimoria that the cheque would be ready the next day. And the next. And the next.

This was embarrassing, but was also normal. Although Mr Swami worked for the son of one of the richest men in the country, Adityasaahab's rule was: One more month in my account. So Mr Swami spent most of his workday telling people that the cheque would be coming the next day. No one believed him, but he said it anyway and listened to their abuse and sly digs at his accent and to their sarcastic responses; and he went on working.

Mr Billimoria was different. He had not shouted. He had not mocked. He always started the conversation with, 'How are you Mr Swami?'

Mr Swami would say that he was well.

Next he would ask: 'Mrs Swami, is she well?'

After that, 'Quite hot, isn't it?"

To which Mr Swami would say, 'Humidity is also too

much.'

And only when these pleasantries were over would Mr Billimoria ask, 'So is there any good news for me, Mr Swami?'

At first Mr Swami had said, 'Tomorrow, Mr Billimoria, tomorrow.' But he felt that he could not do this to someone who was unfailingly polite, so he had started saying, 'I am so sorry, Mr Billimoria.'

And then Mr Billimoria would say, 'Thank you for your time, Mr Swami.'

Until, finally, one day Adityasaahab signed the cheque and handed it over to Mr Swami as if he were doing his accountant a favour.

'Call up that old fool,' Adityasaahab said.

'That's just his way,' Mr Swami said to himself.

'And remind him to collect his cheque.'

'Just his way,' Mr Swami said to himself, doggedly.

'Let's finish this off.'

'His way…his way…his way,' Mr Swami mumbled to himself as he went back to his desk.

He called Mr Billimoria.

'Hello,' said a quiet and beautiful voice on the other side of the phone line. It was such a quiet and beautiful voice; it could only be a quiet and beautiful woman speaking.

'May I speak to Mr Billimoria, please?'

'Certainly,' said the lady. 'Merwanji…' she called.

'Thank you, Mother,' said Mr Billimoria.

Then he spoke into the phone.

'How are you, Mr Billimoria?' asked Mr Swami.

'Is that Mr Swami?' asked Mr Billimoria.

'Yes, sir.'

'Good morning, Mr Billimoria. How are you today?'

'I am very well, Mr Swami. And how are you?'

'I am well.'

'And Mrs Swami?'

'Saritha Kamakshi is fine,' said Mr Swami.

'Is that her name? How beautiful!' said Mr Billimoria.

'Quite hot today,' said Mr Swami.

'It's the humidity,' said Mr Billimoria, and then he giggled.

Mr Swami giggled too. The other two accountants looked up sharply. Mr Raghunathan, who was three months away from retirement, looked shocked. No one had ever giggled at the Burilla Group's Accounts Department in the last forty years that he had worked there.

The other man in the room, Mr Shah, looked shocked because Mr Raghunathan looked shocked.

Mr Swami ignored both of them. His giggles petered away into a set of little gasps.

'There is good news,' he said. 'There is good news.'

He heard Mr Billimoria gasp as if he had won a lottery. In the middle of the happiness he felt at being able to give his 'phone-friend' the news, Mr Swami also felt a pang. This was Mr Billimoria's money. He was selling his beautiful old bungalow with its lovely Chinese-tiled floors and its pigeons cooing fatly and its parijat tree and its old well and its dry fountain with a cherub. He was probably going to live in a small flat. Yet, he had been made to wait so long that he had begun to treat his rightful dues as if he had won a lottery.

'The cheque?' Mr Billimoria asked.

'It is signed and ready.'

'Jolly good,' said Mr Billimoria.

'So this morning,' Mr Swami told Saritha Kamakshi as he mixed some juice of mango pickle with the rice and curd, 'Mr Billimoria came. He had vacated. All the stuff gone. House empty. Adityasaahab gave him the cheque.'

Mr Swami's hand froze as he remembered.

'That's a considerable sum of money, Mr Billimoria,' said Adityasaahab. 'What are you going to do with it?'

'Well, I thought I would build a small village hospital in memory of my mother in Dahanu,' said Mr Billimoria.

'She has passed on?' Mr Swami said.

Mr Billimoria looked a bit apologetic.

'Well, yes, she died a couple of years ago,' he said.

Saritha Kamakshi was not impressed. She gave her husband a friendly thump on his back, causing him to eject a little blob of curd-rice back into his plate.

'That only? See, we are calling lots of people mother. I am calling your mother Amma or no? He must be calling some other elderly woman in his family like that only.'

The cheque was handed over. Now it was Mr Billimoria's turn to hand over the keys.

'Mr Burilla,' said Mr Billimoria, 'do you mind if I go back one last time today? I have to pick up my cat.'

There was silence.

'Cats,' said Mr Billimoria, 'are very easily spooked. When I emptied the house, it must have seemed like a jungle had been cut down. Like the whole world had changed. So she disappeared into the house somewhere.'

Adityasaahab was silent. It was a ploy he used. Mr Swami had noticed that it was a very effective ploy. A rich man's silence can be a frightening thing. He had learnt, after many years of watching his employer, to be silent as well. Otherwise, he found that he would say what he thought Adityasaahab wanted him to say. He had given up his weekly off once to end a silence; and he had offered to work overtime on Saritha Kamakshi's birthday. Now he had learnt to be silent too. And to pray.

Mr Billimoria seemed accustomed to silence. He sat still and waited. Adityasaahab began to tap his fingers. Everyone in the Burilla Group agreed that this was a bad sign, but Mr Billimoria did not know this. He continued to remain silent as the dull glint of Adityasaahab's fingernails flashed. Finally Adityasaahab spoke.

'Well,' he said. 'Well.'

Then he fell silent again.

Mr Swami began to wonder whether they were going to sit there all day. He coughed gently. Both men looked at him.

'I could go with Mr Billimoria,' he said.

Adityasaahab relaxed visibly.

'Yes, yes,' he said. 'That will be best.'

Mr Billimoria cocked his head. He looked at Mr Swami and it seemed as if he wanted to apologize. Then he sighed again.

'Not the best, but I suppose it will have to do,' he said.

Adityasaahab's eyes glinted.

'Keep an eye,' he said to Mr Swami, as he left in a puff of expensive aftershave and hair gel.

On the way, in his old Fiat, Mr Billimoria asked suddenly: 'What do you think happens to us after we die, Mr Swami?'

Mr Swami had been about to say something about the dust, so he was taken completely unawares.

'In our Vedas, it is said…' he began.

'Yes, yes, and in our Zend Avesta it is said. And in the Koran, something else is said. The Bible says something else. Also the tribals say this happens, that happens. But what do *you* believe?' asked Mr Billimoria.

Mr Swami looked out of the window. He thought of his Mission School, the Ramakrishna Mission. He thought how easy it had been when everyone believed the same thing. Then he had left school, and in college he had met people who believed other things. At first, he had thought, 'They must be wrong.' Later, he thought, 'They may be right.' Next he thought, 'We are all wrong.' Finally, 'Maybe, we are all right.' Then he had got a job and a wife and a mortgage, and he had stopped thinking about these things.

'Forget it,' Mr Billimoria said gruffly. 'In this day and age, such questions are best left unanswered. No, it is better that they are not asked at all. I withdraw the question.'

'What do you believe, Mr Billimoria?' Mr Swami asked.

'I think you find yourself in something like a huge hotel banquet room. And under every gleaming dome is a choice, lying on a very fine porcelain dish. One says, 'I want another life so I can do better.' Another says, 'Judge me now: Heaven or Hell.' A third says, 'I haven't had enough of the world.''

'By golly,' said Mr Swami. 'Much confusion for the Divine Being.'

'Well, if it's a Divine Being, it should not be easy to confuse,' said Mr Billimoria. 'Or why would it have invented so many beetles?'

'Are there many beetles in the world?'

'The great biologist J.B.S. Haldane said that if there was a Creator then he had a distinct fondness for beetles. There are more than 3,00,000 types of beetles.'

Mr Swami had the uncomfortable feeling that Mr Haldane and Mr Billimoria did not believe in the Divine Being. He cast about for another subject, something else to talk about. But he discovered that once you tell yourself 'let's not talk about elephants', only elephants come tramping down, from your mind on to your tongue.

'And what happens to the people who say: "I haven't had enough of this world"?' asked Mr Swami.

'Oh, they become ghosts,' said Mr Billimoria.

The Fiat lurched to a halt. They were at Billimoria House. The sun was bright on their backs. The city played and screamed and crashed and banged and honked and shouted around them. Mr Swami felt cold. At the door, a side door, he asked: 'Yesterday, when I called you, who picked up the phone?'

'My mother?' said Mr Billimonia.

'Your mother' asked Mr Swami. 'I thought...'?

'She died ten years ago. It was very sudden,' said Mr Billimoria.

And then they were in the house. The door closed behind them and the city was cut away, as if by a knife. Silence fell like a silk sari slipping off its hanger in a dark cupboard. Suddenly

Mr Swami felt as if he might be floating. He turned to Mr Billimoria. The old man began to coo and gurgle.

'Billi, Billi,' he called in the high-pitched voice men use for pets they love. Then he chuckled.

'Mori billi,' he called. 'Billimoria ni billi!'

Mr Swami did not know much Gujarati. Just enough to know that Mr Billimoria was calling his cat.

Nothing happened. No breath stirred. No cobwebs sighed. The house, it seemed, was wearing a muffler. He found himself saying this.

'It seems as if the house is wearing a muffler over its eyes and ears.'

'Do you really think so?' asked Mr Billimoria. His voice was reassuringly normal. 'You're right, though. It feels like that.'

The muffler flapped for a moment.

'Billi, billi,' called Mr Billimoria.

'Is that her name?' asked Mr Swami. He felt in himself an urge to keep on talking.

'It is like calling a spade a spade,' he said.

'Indeed,' said Mr Billimoria. 'Here she is. Come Billi, good girl.'

Again Mr Swami felt the stillness shift and tremble.

'Mr Billimoria,' he said, and he was proud that his voice did not tremble. 'I cannot see anything but…'

'But what, Mr Swami?'

'I feel something,' said Mr Swami.

'It's only Billi,' said Mr Billimoria.

'I would like to see her,' said Mr Swami.

'It's only Billi,' said Mr Billimoria.

'I would like to see her,' said Mr Swami.

'Would you?' asked Mr Billimoria. 'Are you sure?'

Mr Swami was sure. His eyes seemed to be full of an odd fog.

'Billi,' ordered Mr Billimoria. 'Show.'

A tiger appeared.

'Jagadeeshwara!' shouted Mr Swami.

'Naughty cat,' said Mr Billimoria and snapped his fingers at the tiger who yawned, stretched and shrank to an ordinary tabby.

'How? How?'

'I believe the ghost body is malleable,' said Mr Billimoria, as if he were talking of a recipe for an omelette. 'You spend most of your time in the form you enjoyed most or in the form you thought of yourself the most. So if you enjoyed being a schoolboy, that's who you will be as a ghost.'

Something hit Mr Swami on the ear. He turned around, though he did not want to look.

'Pip pip old bean,' said a cheeky schoolboy.

'That's grand-uncle Pesi,' said Mr Billimoria.

'Peshotan, enough of that,' said a familiar voice.

'Mother?' said Mr Billimoria.

'*I didn't know where to look,*' said Mr Swami to Saritha Kamakshi. '*There was a fulsome woman in a revealing bathing dress.*'

'*Parsi women are all…*'

'*Please,*' said Mr Swami. '*We must not talk about communities as if they are all the same. That is stereotyping and it leads to communal hatred.'*

'Well,' said Saritha Kamakshi. 'That Parsi woman was a ghost?'

'Oh, there were many, many of them,' said Mr Swami.

Uncle Pesi kept waxing and waning. When he spoke to Mrs Billimoria he became a cranky old man and she became a woman with silvery grey hair in a dressing gown. When they turned to speak to him, Peshotan became Pesi and Mrs Billimoria became a woman in a bathing suit.

'Pesi took me driving in his car,' said Mrs Billimoria. 'He had an argument with Rampart Row. He lost.'

And others kept coming out of the woodwork it seemed. There was a little girl, clutching her doll.

'She died of meningitis when there were no steroids,' said Mr Billimoria.

'Hello, I'm Nanthee,' said the girl, smiling sweetly. Then she lay down and began to swell up and swear. Then she started screaming.

'You can stay here, Nancy,' said Mr Billimoria.

'Oh good,' said Nancy and vanished.

'Stay here?' Mr Swami said.

'Are we staying too?' Uncle Pesi asked.

'No,' said Mr Billimoria.

'Get into the car.'

'I could stay for a while...' whined Uncle Pesi. 'I could do a really good job.'

'You don't have the stomach for a haunting,' said Mr Billimoria. 'Hurry up. We can't waste Mr Swami's time.'

The ghosts kept drifting in. First came an aunt who wanted

to tell him about her meeting with aapro Zubin, the famous conductor who had asked her why she was hiding her gift at the piano. Another middle-aged lady, who thought she had lost a recipe for dhansak that her mother had given her, came in. She wanted a few more hours to search the house.

'You can stay and look for as long as you like,' said Mr Billimoria.

'Thank you Merwanji,' said the lady and drifted off.

'You are leaving her behind?' said Mr Swami, slightly shocked.

'Yes,' said Mr Billimoria airily.

'Why?'

'I have decided that I should leave Mr Burilla a little gift. A few people to warm his house until he takes over.'

'These...'

'These ghosts, yes.'

'Merwanji...' came a familiar voice.

It was Mrs Billimoria, only now she was dressed in blue skirt and coat with a white shirt underneath.

'Yes, Mother?'

'It was my idea, Mr Swami,' she said. 'My Merwanji is far too kind. But when I heard that Adityasaahab was not paying, I told him, let's leave him a little gift. One ghost for each day the cheque is delayed.'

***

When Mr Swami got back to the office, Adityasaahab asked, 'Did he try to take anything with him?'

'No, only his cat,' said Mr Swami. In his head, he thought,

'He left many things behind, though.'

Mr Swami began to giggle. But as he sat at his desk, he began to wonder. Finally, he called Mr Billimoria's mobile phone.

Mr Billimoria answered.

'If there are ghosts in your house, would there be ghosts in mine?' he asked.

'Oh, only if your home is more than a hundred years old,' said Mr Billimoria airily.

It was Saritha Kamakshi's turn to go pale. She looked around at the high roof and the teak doors, the windows so old that the glass was thicker at the bottom than at the top since it had flowed downwards over the years.

'*How did he do it?' she demanded. 'What did he say to the cat?'*

'*He said "show",' said Mr Swami and snapped his fingers.*

'*Show,' said Saritha and snapped her fingers before Mr Swami could stop her, and one by one they began to appear.*

Rip Van Winkle

Washington Irving

Whoever has made a voyage up the Hudson must remember the Catskill Mountains. They are a dismembered branch of the great Appalachian family, and are seen away to the west of the river, swelling up to a noble height, and lording it over the surrounding country. Every change of season, every change of weather, indeed, every hour of the day, produces some change in the magical hues and shapes of these mountains, and they are regarded by all the good wives, far and near, as perfect barometers. When the weather is fair and settled, they are clothed in blue and purple, and print their bold outlines on the clear evening sky; but sometimes, when the rest of the landscape is cloudless, they will gather a hood of grey vapours about their summits, which, in the last rays of the setting sun, will glow and light up like a crown of glory.

At the foot of these fairy mountains the voyager may have descried the light smoke curling up from a village whose shingle roofs gleam among the trees, just where the blue tints of the upland melt away into the fresh green of the nearer landscape. It is a little village of great antiquity, having been founded by some of the Dutch colonists, in the early times of the province, just about the beginning of the government of the good Peter Stuyvesant (may he rest in peace!), and there were some of the houses of the original settlers standing within a few years, with lattice windows, gable fronts surmounted with weathercocks, and built of small yellow bricks brought from Holland.

In that same village, and in one of these very houses (which, to tell the precise truth, was sadly time-worn and weather-beaten), there lived many years since, while the country was yet a province of Great Britain, a simple, good-natured fellow, of the name of Rip Van Winkle. He was a descendant of the Van Winkles who figured so gallantly in the chivalrous days of Peter Stuyvesant, and accompanied him to the siege of Fort Christina.

He inherited, however, but little of the martial character of his ancestors. I have observed that he was a simple, good-natured man; he was, moreover, a kind neighbour and an obedient, henpecked husband. Indeed, to the latter circumstance might be owing that meekness of spirit which gained him such universal popularity; for those men are most apt to be obsequious and conciliating abroad who are under the discipline of shrews at home. Their tempers, doubtless, are rendered pliant and malleable in the fiery furnace of domestic tribulation, and a curtain lecture is worth all the sermons in the world for teaching the virtues of patience and long-suffering. A termagant wife may, therefore, in some respects, be considered a tolerable blessing; and if so, Rip Van Winkle was thrice blessed.

Certain it is that he was a great favourite among all the good wives of the village, who, as usual with the amiable sex, took his part in all family squabbles, and never failed, whenever they talked those matters over in their evening gossipings, to lay all the blame on Dame Van Winkle. The children of the village, too, would shout with joy whenever he approached. He assisted at their sports, made their playthings, taught them to fly kites and shoot marbles, and told them long stories of ghosts, witches, and Indians. Whenever he went dodging about the village, he was surrounded by a troop of them, hanging on his skirts, clambering on his back, and playing a thousand tricks on him with impunity; and not a dog would bark at him throughout the neighbourhood.

The great error in Rip's composition was an insuperable aversion to all kinds of profitable labour. It could not be from the want of assiduity or perseverance; for he would sit on a wet rock, with a rod as long and heavy as a Tartar's lance, and fish all day without a murmur, even though he should not be encouraged by a single nibble. He would carry a fowling piece on his shoulder, for hours together, trudging through woods and swamps, and up hill and down dale, to shoot a few squirrels or wild pigeons. He would never even refuse to assist a neighbour in the roughest toil, and was a foremost man at all country frolics for husking Indian corn, or building stone fences. The women of the village, too, used to employ him to run their errands, and to do such little odd jobs as their less obliging husbands would not do for them; in a word, Rip was ready to attend to anybody's business but his own; but as to doing family duty, and keeping his farm in order, it was impossible.

In fact, he declared it was of no use to work on his farm; it was the most pestilent little piece of ground in the whole country; everything about it went wrong, and would go wrong, in spite of him. His fences were continually falling to pieces; his cow would either go astray or get among the cabbages; weeds were sure to grow quicker in his fields than anywhere else; the rain always made a point of setting in just as he had some outdoor work to do; so that though his patrimonial estate had dwindled away under his management, acre by acre, until there was little more left than a mere patch of Indian corn and potatoes, yet it was the worst-conditioned farm in the neighbourhood.

His children, too, were as ragged and wild as if they belonged to nobody. His son Rip, an urchin begotten in his own likeness, promised to inherit the habits, with the old clothes of his father. He was generally seen trooping like a colt at his mother's heels, equipped in a pair of his father's cast-off galligaskins, which he had much ado to hold up with one hand, as a fine lady does her train in bad weather.

Rip Van Winkle, however, was one of those happy mortals, of foolish, well-oiled dispositions, who take the world easy, eat white bread or brown, whichever can be got with least thought or trouble, and would rather starve on a penny than work for a pound. If left to himself, he would have whistled life away, in perfect contentment; but his wife kept continually dinning in his ears about his idleness, his carelessness, and the ruin he was bringing on his family. Morning, noon, and night, her tongue was incessantly going, and everything he said or did was sure to produce a torrent of household eloquence. Rip had but one way of replying to all lectures of the kind, and that, by frequent use, had grown into a habit. He shrugged his shoulders, shook his head, cast up his eyes, but said nothing. This, however, always provoked a fresh volley from his wife, so that he was fain to draw off his forces, and take to the outside of the house—the only side which, in truth, belongs to a henpecked husband.

Rip's sole domestic adherent was his dog Wolf, who was as much henpecked as his master; for Dame Van Winkle regarded them as companions in idleness, and even looked upon Wolf with an evil eye, as the cause of his master's so often going astray. True it is, in all points of spirit befitting an honourable dog, he was as courageous an animal as ever scoured the woods—but what courage can withstand the ever-going and all-besetting terrors of a woman's tongue? The moment Wolf entered the house his crest fell, his tail drooped to the ground, or curled between his legs; he sneaked about with a gallows air, casting many a sidelong glance at Dame Van Winkle, and at the least flourish of a broomstick or ladle would fly to the door with yelping precipitation.

Times grew worse and worse with Rip Van Winkle as years of matrimony rolled on; a tart temper never mellows with age, and a sharp tongue is the only edged tool that grows keener by constant use. For a long while he used to console himself, when driven from home, by frequenting a kind of perpetual club of the sages, philosophers, and other idle personages of the village, which held its sessions on a bench before a small inn, designated by a rubicund portrait of His Majesty George the Third. Here they used to sit in the shade, of a long lazy summer's day, talking listlessly over village gossip, or telling endless sleepy stories about nothing. But it would have been worth any statesman's money to have heard the profound discussions which sometimes took place, when by chance an old newspaper fell into their hands, from some passing traveller. How solemnly they would listen to the contents, as drawled out by Derrick Van Bummel, the schoolmaster, a dapper, learned little man, who was not to be daunted by the most gigantic word in the dictionary; and how sagely they would deliberate upon public events some months after they had taken place.

The opinions of this junto were completely controlled by Nicholas Vedder, a patriarch of the village, and landlord of the inn, at the door of which he took his seat from morning till night, just moving sufficiently to avoid the sun, and keep in the shade of a large tree; so that the neighbours could tell the hour by his movements as accurately as by a sundial. It is true, he was rarely heard to speak, but smoked his pipe incessantly. His adherents, however (for every great man has his adherents), perfectly understood him, and knew how to gather his opinions. When anything that was read or related displeased him, he was observed to smoke his pipe vehemently, and send forth short, frequent, and angry puffs; but when pleased, he would inhale the smoke slowly and tranquilly, and emit it in light and placid clouds, and sometimes taking the pipe from his mouth, and letting the fragrant vapour curl about his nose, would gravely nod his head in token of perfect approbation.

From even this stronghold the unlucky Rip was at length routed by his termagant wife, who would suddenly break in upon the tranquillity of the assemblage, and call the members all to nought; nor was that august personage, Nicholas Vedder himself, sacred from the daring tongue of this terrible virago, who charged him outright with encouraging her husband in habits of idleness.

Poor Rip was at last reduced almost to despair; and his only alternative, to escape from the labour of the farm and clamour of his wife, was to take gun in hand and stroll away into the woods. Here he would sometimes seat himself at the foot of a tree, and share the contents of his wallet with Wolf, with whom he sympathized as a fellow-sufferer in persecution. 'Poor Wolf,' he would say, 'thy mistress leads thee a dog's life of it; but never mind, my lad, while I live thou shalt never want a friend to stand by thee!' Wolf would wag his tail, look wistfully in his master's face, and if dogs can feel pity, I verily believe he reciprocated the sentiment with all his heart.

In a long ramble of the kind on a fine autumnal day, Rip had unconsciously scrambled to one of the highest parts of the Catskill Mountains. He was after his favourite sport of squirrel shooting, and the still solitudes had echoed and re-echoed with the reports of his gun. Panting and fatigued, he threw himself, late in the afternoon, on a green knoll, covered with mountain herbage, that crowned the brow of a precipice. From an opening between the trees he could overlook all the lower country for many a mile of rich woodland. He saw at a distance the lordly Hudson, far, far below him, moving on its silent but majestic course, the reflection of a purple cloud, or the sail of a lagging bark, here and there sleeping on its glassy bosom, and at last losing itself in the blue highlands.

On the other side he looked down into a deep mountain glen, wild, lonely, and shagged, the bottom filled with fragments from the impending cliffs, and scarcely lighted by the reflected rays of the setting sun. For some time Rip lay musing on this scene; evening was gradually advancing; the mountains began to throw their long blue shadows over the valleys; he saw that it would be dark long before he could reach the village, and he heaved a heavy sigh when he thought of encountering the terrors of Dame Van Winkle.

As he was about to descend, he heard a voice from a distance, hallooing, 'Rip Van Winkle! Rip Van Winkle!' He looked around, but could see nothing but a crow winging its solitary flight across the mountain. He thought his fancy must have deceived him, and turned again to descend, when he heard the same cry ring through the still evening air: 'Rip Van Winkle! Rip Van Winkle!'—at the same time Wolf bristled up his back, and giving a low growl, skulked to his master's side, looking fearfully down into the glen. Rip now felt a vague apprehension stealing over him; he looked anxiously in the same direction, and perceived a strange figure slowly toiling up the rocks, and bending under the weight of something he carried on his back. He was surprised to see any human being in this lonely and unfrequented place, but supposing it to be some one of the neighbourhood in need of assistance, he hastened down to yield it.

On nearer approach, he was still more surprised at the singularity of the stranger's appearance. He was a short, square-built old fellow, with thick bushy hair, and a grizzled beard. His dress was of the antique Dutch fashion—a cloth jerkin strapped around the waist—several pair of breeches, the outer one of ample volume, decorated with rows of buttons down the sides, and bunches at the knees. He bore on his shoulders a stout keg, that seemed full of liquor, and made signs for Rip to approach and assist him with the load.

Though rather shy and distrustful of this new acquaintance, Rip complied with his usual alacrity, and mutually relieving one another, they clambered up a narrow gully, apparently the dry bed of a mountain torrent. As they ascended, Rip every now and then heard long rolling peals, like distant thunder, that seemed to issue out of a deep ravine, or rather cleft between lofty rocks, toward which their rugged path conducted. He paused for an instant, but supposing it to be the muttering of one of those transient thunder showers which often take place in mountain heights, he proceeded. Passing through the ravine, they came to a hollow, like a small amphitheatre, surrounded by perpendicular precipices, over the brinks of which impending trees shot their branches, so that you only caught glimpses of the azure sky and the bright evening cloud. During the whole time, Rip and his companion had laboured on in silence; for though the former marvelled greatly what could be the object of carrying a keg of liquor up this wild mountain, yet there was something strange and incomprehensible about the unknown that inspired awe and checked familiarity.

On entering the amphitheatre, new objects of wonder presented themselves. On a level spot in the centre was a company of odd-looking personages playing at ninepins. They were dressed in a quaint, outlandish fashion: some wore short doublets, others jerkins, with long knives in their belts, and most had enormous breeches, of similar style with that of the guide's. Their visages, too, were peculiar: one had a large head, broad face, and small, piggish eyes; the face of another seemed to consist entirely of nose, and was surmounted by a white sugar-loaf hat set off with a little red cock's tail. They all had beards, of various shapes and colours. There was one who seemed to be the commander. He was a stout old gentleman, with a weather-beaten countenance; he wore a laced doublet, broad belt and hanger, high-crowned hat and feather, red stockings, and high-heeled shoes, with roses in them. The whole group reminded Rip of the figures in an old Flemish painting, in the parlour of Dominie Van Schaick, the village parson, and which had been brought over from Holland at the time of the settlement.

What seemed particularly odd to Rip, was that though these folks were evidently amusing themselves, yet they maintained the gravest faces, the most mysterious silence, and were, withal, the most melancholy party of pleasure he had ever witnessed. Nothing interrupted the stillness of the scene but the noise of the balls, which, whenever they were rolled, echoed along the mountains like rumbling peals of thunder.

As Rip and his companion approached them, they suddenly desisted from their play, and stared at him with such fixed statue-like gaze, and such strange, uncouth, lacklustre countenances, that his heart turned within him, and his knees smote together. His companion now emptied the contents of the keg into large flagons, and made signs to him to wait upon the company. He obeyed with fear and trembling; they quaffed the liquor in profound silence, and then returned to their game.

By degrees, Rip's awe and apprehension subsided. He even ventured, when no eye was fixed upon him, to taste the beverage, which he found had much of the flavour of excellent Hollands. He was naturally a thirsty soul, and was soon tempted to repeat the draught. One taste provoked another, and he reiterated his visits to the flagon so often, that at length his senses were overpowered, his eyes swam in his head, his head gradually declined, and he fell into a deep sleep.

On awaking, he found himself on the green knoll from whence he had first seen the old man of the glen. He rubbed his eyes—it was a bright sunny morning. The birds were hopping and twittering among the bushes, and the eagle was wheeling aloft and breasting the pure mountain breeze. 'Surely,' thought Rip, 'I have not slept here all night.' He recalled the occurrences before he fell asleep. The strange man with a keg of liquor—the mountain ravine—the wild retreat among the rocks—the woe-begone party at ninepins—the flagon—'Oh! that flagon! that wicked flagon!' thought Rip—'what excuse shall I make to Dame Van Winkle?'

He looked round for his gun, but in place of the clean, well-oiled fowling piece, he found an old firelock lying by him, the barrel incrusted with rust, the lock falling off, and the stock worm-eaten. He now suspected that the grave roysters of the mountain had put a trick upon him, and having dosed him with liquor, had robbed him of his gun. Wolf, too, had disappeared, but he might have strayed away after a squirrel or partridge. He whistled after him, shouted his name, but all in vain; the echoes repeated his whistle and shout, but no dog was to be seen.

He determined to revisit the scene of the last evening's gambol, and if he met with any of the party, to demand his dog and gun. As he rose to walk, he found himself stiff in the joints, and wanting in his usual activity. 'These mountain beds do not agree with me,' thought Rip, 'and if this frolic should lay me up with a fit of the rheumatism, I shall have a blessed time with Dame Van Winkle.' With some difficulty he got down into the glen; he found the gully up which he and his companion had ascended the preceding evening; but to his astonishment a mountain stream was now foaming down it, leaping from rock to rock, and filling the glen with babbling murmurs. He, however, made shift to scramble up its sides, working his toilsome way through thickets of birch, sassafras, and witch-hazel, and sometimes tripped up or entangled by the wild grape vines that twisted their coils and tendrils from tree to tree, and spread a kind of network in his path.

At length he reached to where the ravine had opened through the cliffs to the amphitheatre; but no traces of such opening remained. The rocks presented a high, impenetrable wall, over which the torrent came tumbling in a sheet of feathery foam, and fell into a broad, deep basin, black from the shadows of the surrounding forest. Here, then, poor Rip was brought to a stand. He again called and whistled after his dog; he was only answered by the cawing of a flock of idle crows, sporting high in air about a dry tree that overhung a sunny precipice; and who, secure in their elevation, seemed to look down and scoff at the poor man's perplexities. What was to be done? The morning was passing away, and Rip felt famished for want of his breakfast. He grieved to give up his dog and gun; he dreaded to meet his wife; but it would not do to starve among the mountains. He shook his head, shouldered the rusty firelock, and, with a heart full of trouble and anxiety, turned his steps homeward.

As he approached the village, he met a number of people, but none whom he knew, which somewhat surprised him, for he had thought himself acquainted with everyone in the country round. Their dress, too, was of a different fashion from that to which he was accustomed. They all stared at him with equal marks of surprise, and whenever they cast their eyes upon him, invariably stroked their chins. The constant recurrence of this gesture induced Rip, involuntarily, to do the same, when, to his astonishment, he found his beard had grown a foot long!

He had now entered the skirts of the village. A troop of strange children ran at his heels, hooting after him, and pointing at his grey beard. The dogs, too, none of which he recognized for his old acquaintances, barked at him as he passed. The very village was altered: it was larger and more populous. There were rows of houses which he had never seen before, and those which had been his familiar haunts had disappeared. Strange names were over the doors—strange faces at the windows—everything was strange. His mind now began to misgive him; he doubted whether both he and the world around him were not bewitched. Surely this was his native village, which he had left but the day before. There stood the Catskill Mountains—there ran the silver Hudson at a distance—there was every hill and dale precisely as it had always been—Rip was sorely perplexed—'That flagon last night,' thought he, 'has addled my poor head sadly!'

It was with some difficulty that he found the way to his own house, which he approached with silent awe, expecting every moment to hear the shrill voice of Dame Van Winkle. He found the house gone to decay—the roof fallen in, the windows shattered, and the doors off the hinges. A half-starved dog, that looked like Wolf, was skulking about it. Rip called him by name, but the cur snarled, showed his teeth, and passed on. This was an unkind cut indeed—'My very dog,' sighed poor Rip, 'has forgotten me!'

He entered the house, which, to tell the truth, Dame Van Winkle had always kept in neat order. It was empty, forlorn, and apparently abandoned. This desolateness overcame all his connubial fears—he called loudly for his wife and children—the lonely chambers rung for a moment with his voice, and then all again was silence.

He now hurried forth, and hastened to his old resort, the little village inn—but it too was gone. A large rickety wooden building stood in its place, with great gaping windows, some of them broken, and mended with old hats and petticoats, and over the door was painted, 'The Union Hotel, by Jonathan

Doolittle.' Instead of the great tree which used to shelter the quiet little Dutch inn of yore, there now was reared a tall naked pole, with something on the top that looked like a red nightcap, and from it was fluttering a flag, on which was a singular assemblage of stars and stripes—all this was strange and incomprehensible. He recognized on the sign, however, the ruby face of King George, under which he had smoked so many a peaceful pipe, but even this was singularly metamorphosed. The red coat was changed for one of blue and buff, a sword was stuck in the hand instead of a scepter, the head was decorated with a cocked hat, and underneath was painted in large characters, GENERAL WASHINGTON.

There was, as usual, a crowd of folk about the door, but none whom Rip recollected. The very character of the people seemed changed. There was a busy, bustling, disputatious tone about it, instead of the accustomed phlegm and drowsy tranquillity. He looked in vain for the sage Nicholas Vedder, with his broad face, double chin, and fair long pipe, uttering clouds of tobacco smoke instead of idle speeches; or Van Bummel, the schoolmaster, doling forth the contents of an ancient newspaper. In place of these, a lean, bilious-looking fellow, with his pockets full of handbills, was haranguing vehemently about rights of citizens—election—members of Congress—liberty—Bunker's Hill—heroes of '76—and other words, that were a perfect Babylonish jargon to the bewildered Van Winkle.

The appearance of Rip, with his long grizzled beard, his rusty fowling piece, his uncouth dress, and the army of women and children that had gathered at his heels, soon attracted the attention of the tavern politicians. They crowded around him, eying him from head to foot, with great curiosity. The orator bustled up to him, and drawing him partly aside, inquired 'on which side he voted?' Rip stared in vacant stupidity. Another short but busy little fellow pulled him by the arm, and raising on tiptoe, inquired in his ear, 'whether he was Federal or Democrat.' Rip was equally at a loss to comprehend the question; when a knowing, self-important old gentleman, in a sharp cocked hat, made his way through the crowd, putting them to the right and left with his elbows as he passed, and planting himself before Van Winkle, with one arm akimbo, the other resting on his cane, his keen eyes and sharp hat penetrating, as it were, into his very soul, demanded, in an austere tone, 'what brought him to the election with a gun on his shoulder, and a mob at his heels, and whether he meant to breed a riot in the village?' 'Alas! Gentlemen,' cried Rip, somewhat dismayed, 'I am a poor quiet man, a native of the place, and a loyal subject of the king, God bless him!'

Here a general shout burst from the bystanders—'A Tory! A Tory! A spy! A refugee! Hustle him! Away with him!' It was with great difficulty that the self-important man in the cocked hat restored order; and having assumed a tenfold austerity of brow, demanded again of the unknown culprit, what he came there for, and whom he was seeking. The poor man humbly assured him that he meant no harm; but merely came there in search of some of his neighbours, who used to keep about the tavern.

'Well—who are they?—name them.'

Rip bethought himself a moment, and then inquired,

'Where's Nicholas Vedder?'

There was silence for a little while, when an old man replied in a thin, piping voice, 'Nicholas Vedder? Why, he is dead and gone these eighteen years! There was a wooden tombstone in the churchyard that used to tell all about him, but that's rotted and gone, too.'

'Where's Brom Dutcher?'

'Oh, he went off to the army in the beginning of the war; some say he was killed at the battle of Stony Point—others say he was drowned in a squall, at the foot of Antony's Nose. I don't know—he never came back again.'

'Where's Van Bummel, the schoolmaster?'

'He went off to the wars, too, was a great militia general, and is now in Congress.'

Rip's heart died away, at hearing of these sad changes in his home and friends, and finding himself thus alone in the world. Every answer puzzled him, too, by treating of such enormous lapses of time, and of matters which he could not understand: war—Congress—Stony Point!—he had no courage to ask after any more friends, but cried out in despair, 'Does nobody here know Rip Van Winkle?'

'Oh, Rip Van Winkle!' exclaimed two or three, 'Oh, to be sure! That's Rip Van Winkle yonder, leaning against the tree.'

Rip looked, and beheld a precise counterpart of himself, as he went up the mountain: apparently as lazy, and certainly as ragged. The poor fellow was now completely confounded. He doubted his own identity, and whether he was himself or another man. In the midst of his bewilderment, the man in the cocked hat demanded who he was, and what was his name?

'God knows,' exclaimed he, at his wit's end; 'I'm not myself—I'm somebody else—that's me yonder—no—that's somebody else, got into my shoes—I was myself last night, but I fell asleep on the mountain, and they've changed my gun, and everything's changed, and I'm changed, and I can't tell what's my name, or who I am!'

The bystanders began now to look at each other, nod, wink significantly, and tap their fingers against their foreheads. There was a whisper, also, about securing the gun, and keeping the old fellow from doing mischief; at the very suggestion of which, the self-important man in the cocked hat retired with some precipitation. At this critical moment a fresh, likely woman pressed through the throng to get a peep at the grey-bearded man. She had a chubby child in her arms, which, frightened at his looks, began to cry. 'Hush, Rip,' cried she, 'hush, you little fool, the old man won't hurt you.' The name of the child, the air of the mother, the tone of her voice, all awakened a train of recollections in his mind. 'What is your name, my good woman?' asked he.

'Judith Gardenier.'

'And your father's name?'

'Ah, poor man, his name was Rip Van Winkle; it's twenty years since he went away from home with his gun, and never has been heard of since—his dog came home without him; but whether he shot himself, or was carried away by the Indians, nobody can tell. I was then but a little girl.'

Rip had but one question more to ask; but he put it with a faltering voice:—

'Where's your mother?'

'Oh, she too had died but a short time since; she broke a blood vessel in a fit of passion at a New England peddler.'

There was a drop of comfort, at least, in this intelligence. The honest man could contain himself no longer.—He caught his daughter and her child in his arms.—'I am your father!' cried he—'Young Rip Van Winkle once—old Rip Van Winkle now!—Does nobody know poor Rip Van Winkle!'

All stood amazed, until an old woman, tottering out from among the crowd, put her hand to her brow, and peering under it in his face for a moment, exclaimed, 'Sure enough! it is Rip Van Winkle—it is himself. Welcome home again, old neighbour.—Why, where have you been these twenty long years?'

Rip's story was soon told, for the whole twenty years had been to him but as one night. The neighbours stared when they heard it; some were seen to wink at each other, and put their tongues in their cheeks; and the self-important man in the cocked hat, who, when the alarm was over, had returned to the field, screwed down the corners of his mouth, and shook his head—upon which there was a general shaking of the head throughout the assemblage.

It was determined, however, to take the opinion of old Peter Vanderdonk, who was seen slowly advancing up the road. He was a descendant of the historian of that name, who wrote one of the earliest accounts of the province. Peter was the most ancient inhabitant of the village, and well versed in all the wonderful events and traditions of the neighbourhood. He recollected Rip at once, and corroborated his story in the most satisfactory manner. He assured the company that it was a fact, handed down from his ancestor the historian, that the Catskill Mountains had always been haunted by strange beings. That it was affirmed that the great Hendrick Hudson, the first discoverer of the river and country, kept a kind of vigil there every twenty years, with his crew of the *Half-Moon,* being permitted in this way to revisit the scenes of his enterprise, and keep a guardian eye upon the river, and the great city called by his name. That his father had once seen them in their old Dutch dresses playing at ninepins in a hollow of the mountain; and that he himself had heard, one summer afternoon, the sound of their balls, like long peals of thunder.

To make a long story short, the company broke up, and returned to the more important concerns of the election. Rip's daughter took him home to live with her; she had a snug, well-furnished house, and a stout cheery farmer for a husband, whom Rip recollected for one of the urchins that used to climb upon his back. As to Rip's son and heir, who was the ditto of himself, seen leaning against the tree, he was employed to work on the farm; but evinced an hereditary disposition to attend to anything else but his business.

Rip now resumed his old walks and habits; he soon found many of his former cronies, though all rather the worse for the wear and tear of time; and preferred making friends among the rising generation, with whom he soon grew into great favour.

Having nothing to do at home, and being arrived at that happy age when a man can do nothing with impunity, he took his place once more on the bench, at the inn door, and was reverenced as one of the patriarchs of the village, and a chronicle of the old times 'before the war.' It was some time before he could get into the regular track of gossip, or could be made to comprehend the strange events that had taken place during his torpor. How that there had been a revolutionary war—that the country had thrown off the yoke of old England—and that, instead of being a subject of His Majesty George III, he was now a free citizen of the United States. Rip, in fact, was no politician; the changes of states and empires made but little impression on him; but there was one species of despotism under which he had long groaned, and that was—petticoat government; happily, that was at an end; he had got his neck out of the yoke of matrimony, and could go in and out whenever he pleased, without dreading the tyranny of Dame Van Winkle. Whenever her name was mentioned, however, he shook his head, shrugged his shoulders, and cast up his eyes; which might pass either for an expression of resignation to his fate, or joy at his deliverance.

He used to tell his story to every stranger that arrived at Dr Doolittle's hotel. He was observed, at first, to vary on some points every time he told it, which was, doubtless, owing to his having so recently awaked. It at last settled down precisely to the tale I have related, and not a man, woman, or child in the neighbourhood but knew it by heart. Some always pretended to doubt the reality of it, and insisted that Rip had been out of his head, and this was one point on which he always remained flighty. The old Dutch inhabitants, however, almost universally gave it full credit. Even to this day they never hear a thunderstorm of a summer afternoon, about the Catskills, but they say Hendrick Hudson and his crew are at their game of ninepins; and it is a common wish of all henpecked husbands in the neighbourhood, when life hangs heavy on their hands, that they might have a quieting draught out of Rip Van Winkle's flagon.